SARANORMAL

Playing with Fire

by Phoebe Rivers

SIMON SPOTLIGHT
New York London Toronto Sydney New Delhi

This book is a work of fiction. Any references to historical events, real people, or real places are used fictitiously. Other names, characters, places, and events are products of the author's imagination, and any resemblance to actual events or places or persons, living or dead, is entirely coincidental.

SIMON SPOTLIGHT
An imprint of Simon & Schuster Children's Publishing Division
1230 Avenue of the Americas, New York, New York 10020

Text by Heather Alexander
For information about special discounts for bulk purchases, please contact Simon & Schuster Special Sales at 1-866-506-1949 or business@simonandschuster.com.
Manufactured in the United States of America 0713 FFG
First Edition 10 9 8 7 6 5 4 3 2 1
ISBN 978-1-4424-8305-7 (pbk)
ISBN 978-1-4424-8306-4 (hc)
ISBN 978-1-4424-8307-1 (eBook)
Library of Congress Catalog Card Number 2012953915

Chapter 1

The front door swung open, taking me by surprise. I sucked in my breath, startled to see him.

To see him with Lily.

I'd just jogged up the Randazzos' walkway. I hadn't yet reached out my hand to ring the bell, and there he was.

His green eyes sparkled with recognition. I did everything to keep my lips from curling in a smile. We held a secretive gaze for a moment, before I looked away.

After all this time, it was strange to see him in front of me. No longer just words illuminated on a tiny screen.

"Sara!" Lily cried. She hadn't been expecting me, but it was a hot day in August and I was bored. It was the kind of day meant for showing up at your best friend's door "This is great. Mason's here."

"Hey there," I said softly as I shifted my weight uncomfortably.

"Mason's hanging out with Buddy," Lily continued. Her little brown dog panted beside Mason's ankle. Buddy had been Mason's dog, but his mom was allergic so Lily's family had taken Buddy in. "His mom dropped him off while she went to the doctor."

Dr. Shiffer, I wanted to say. He specializes in migraines. Mrs. Meyer has been getting superbad headaches lately, and Mason has to watch his brother and sister. Mason's mom heard about Dr. Shiffer from a friend and is hoping he will be able to help her.

But I couldn't say that.

I couldn't say that and not say a whole lot more.

"Sara and I've spent the whole summer on the beach," Lily told Mason, not knowing that Mason already knew that. That Mason knew pretty much everything that was going on with me. She pointed to the black Nikon camera I wore around my neck. "She's been doing this thing where she takes a photo of the same spot on the boardwalk every day at three thirty. Same background but always different people doing different things."

"Really?" Mason actually sounded surprised. As if he knew nothing about my hobby. As if he didn't call me

"Eye Spy" in our texts. "What are you doing with them?"

"She's been printing out the photos," Lily answered. "She's going to mount them on a large board—"

"Actually, I'm thinking of binding them together and making a kind of flip book," I interjected. I fixed my gaze on my orange sandals. I couldn't look at Mason. The flip book had been his idea yesterday.

"Oh, I love it!" Lily's maple-syrup-brown eyes widened. "You could sell that at one of Stellamar's souvenir shops, you know. Print a lot of them. Mason, isn't that totally original?"

"Totally." Mason smirked. "One-of-a-kind. I can't believe *you* thought of that, Sara."

He thought he was being funny, but he wasn't. I smiled my biggest smile back at him, playing along. I was confident he wouldn't dare spill our secret. He knew Lily could never know about us.

If she knew, she'd ask questions.

Questions neither of us wanted to answer.

My stomach twisted. I felt bad. Lily Randazzo was my best friend. She'd be humiliated if she knew Mason and I were playing at barely knowing each other.

I also knew what Lily would think if she found out

that we'd been texting almost every day for the last month. She'd think we liked each other. She'd think we were together.

But we aren't.

We're just friends. There was no way Lily or any of our other friends would believe me. I didn't text with any other boys. Plus, Mason wasn't even from our school. He lived almost thirty minutes away. And he was cute. Really cute. White-blond hair. Tanned skin. Wide-set eyes.

If I didn't like him, she'd want to know what I was doing. Why I was talking all the time to a supercute guy. Guys and girls our age usually don't talk all the time unless they like each other. She'd want to know what we possibly could be talking about.

And the answer to that question was complicated.

Mason unzipped the black backpack that he'd slung over one shoulder. Kneeling in the grass, he searched several outside pockets while rubbing Buddy. The little dog rolled eagerly onto his back, pointing his four paws toward the blue August sky.

"Hey, Lily, I think I left my house keys on your kitchen table," Mason said suddenly. "My mom's going to be here in a minute. Could you see if they're there? I don't want to leave Buddy-boy." He scratched the pale pink skin of Buddy's belly.

Lily shrugged. "Sure." Her long, dark hair swung as she hurried into her house, leaving me and Mason outside together.

"I did it." He stopped petting Buddy and stood so he was close to me.

"Did what?" I shifted back. My bare legs pressed against the lavender blooms of a hydrangea bush. Big hedges and tall flowering bushes bordered the front of Lily's house.

"She's inside." Mason had noticed my eyes dart nervously toward the front door. "She can't hear us. I told my parents."

I gazed blankly at him, my mind still on Lily.

"Sara, I told them. I did it."

The urgency in his voice jolted me. "Really?" I squealed. I couldn't believe it. I'd been pushing Mason for weeks to tell them, but I never thought he'd find the courage to do it. "What happened?"

"Last night after my baseball game, it happened again. I'd pitched nine innings and I was tired, you know? My body was tired, but my brain was more tired—tired of lying and always having to come up with a story to explain it. So when the Gatorade slid across the table, I just blurted it out."

"What'd you say?"

"I told my mom that I moved the drink. Not with my hand or a string but with my mind." Mason's eyes shone. "I told her that I can move objects without touching them. I told her that I've always been able to."

"This is huge!" I was so excited for him. He'd been tortured for so long, having kept his powers a secret from everyone. He'd never meant for me to be the first to find out. We barely knew each other. "What happened next?"

"My mom was skeptical. She went upstairs and had a long talk with my dad." He pushed at the grass with the toe of his worn sneaker. "They came downstairs together. They kept suggesting other explanations. I showed them, but I don't think they can wrap their minds around it yet. You are lucky that your dad understands everything about your powers."

"He's not fully there, believe me."

"I have a feeling there will be a lot more 'little talks,'

as my mom calls them, in our house."

"But they weren't angry, right? They didn't yell or flip out or—"

"No. Can you believe it? They were calm. Surprised. Confused. But no screaming or blaming or any of the other stuff I'd expected."

I had known deep down that Mason's parents wouldn't be mad at him, but he had convinced himself that they would be. That they wouldn't understand. What I knew—what I had learned firsthand, actually, with my own dad—was that sometimes parents don't understand stuff, but that doesn't mean they won't try.

"You need to celebrate," I said, truly happy for him. I pushed back the same strand of straight blond hair that always hung in my eyes so I could see him better.

"Even though I'm not sure what's going to happen next, it feels good to have it out there." Mason scooped Buddy into his arms. "It's your turn now."

"I don't think—"

"Oh no. You're not backing out. We made a pact, Sara," he reminded me. "I tell my parents and you tell Lily."

"It's different," I said.

"It's not," Mason insisted. "My parents rolled with

it when I told them I move objects with the force of my mind. Lily will be cool when you tell her that you can see and talk to ghosts."

"Friends are different from parents," I objected. "Your mom gave birth to you. She's seen you vomit and do stupid things, and no matter what you say or do, she'll always love you. That's what moms and dads do. Friends aren't connected that way. A friend can drop you in a second and never look back."

"You don't believe that about Lily." Mason's gaze turned stern. "Come on, Lily is way cooler and more open-minded than my dad, and if he didn't flip . . . Look, we both know it's been eating at you. Sara, it feels amazing to come clean."

We'd been texting about this for weeks. The very thing that connected us. Our supernatural secrets.

Lily had brought us together at her thirteenth birthday party in June. I'd discovered his power, and then he figured out mine. Maybe because we were so alike in that way, we recognized it in each other.

Besides my family, Mason was the only one I'd ever told. I wanted to tell Lily I saw the dead. All around me. Everywhere.

Lily was the best friend I'd ever had. I knew everything about her. But she knew nothing about me. Nothing important, that is.

But this was big. Huge.

She might laugh at me. She might be afraid of me.

She might not want to be my friend.

The thing was, Lily had seen and heard me do lots of strange things since I moved to Stellamar last summer. She hadn't known there were spirits by my side. I couldn't imagine what she thought.

I couldn't let it go on like this. She'd been so cool. Never questioning me. Always loyal and understanding, no matter how crazy I must've looked.

"I want to tell her." My fingers clenched into fists. "I'm just scared. Petrified, actually."

"Are you sure?" Lily's melodic voice rang out. "I looked everywhere, Mason. No key." As she hurried across the grass, I took a step away from him.

"Really?" Mason patted the pockets of his baggy cargo shorts. "Oops. My bad." He extracted a key, swinging it on a red ribbon. "Must've been here all along."

"What a dummy!" Lily gave him a playful shove, then snatched Buddy from his arms. "Your mom's here." She nodded toward the white SUV that had just pulled up to the curb.

"Later," Mason called, hoisting his backpack onto his shoulder and heading toward the car. Then he turned and caught my eye. *Just do it,* he mouthed.

"Do what?" Lily asked as they drove away. "I saw that, you know. Do what?"

I bit my lip. This was it. The perfect intro. Could I just blurt it out right here?

"Well, he wanted me to . . ." I hesitated. Every time I'd rehearsed this conversation in my mind, we were both in my kitchen and I'd just baked Lily's favorite caramel-swirl brownies. Maybe that didn't matter.

"Honey, do you see the time? We've got to go!"

I gasped as Lily's mom poked her head out from behind the tall hedge to our right. She held a pair of hedge clippers and had a few stray twigs and leaves caught in her long, dark hair.

"What are you doing?" Lily sounded horrified. "Why are you in the bushes?"

"Gardening." Mrs. Randazzo peeled off her floral gardening gloves. "I saw Mason's mom pick him up. We need to get a move on. Lily, you didn't forget the dentist, did you?" From the way Lily scrunched her eyebrows together, I knew she'd definitely forgotten.

"Come on, to the car." Mrs. Randazzo turned to me. "Hi, Sara. Lily can come over after her dentist appointment. You'll have plenty of time together then." Her eyes bored into mine, and suddenly it dawned on me. She'd been in the bushes. Had she heard my conversation with Mason? My breath caught in my throat. I couldn't meet her gaze.

I knew Mrs. Randazzo well enough to know that she wouldn't tell Lily my secret on the way to the dentist. At least I thought she wouldn't.

I cut across the lawns, waving to Mr. Vega, who lived in the gray gabled house that separated my house from Lily's. He was pinning his rosebushes, withering in the heat, to a trellis. I pulled open the back door that led into our kitchen.

Maybe Lily's mom hadn't heard. Or maybe she had.

Either way, I'd made a decision.

I'd tell Lily as soon as she came back.

Chapter 2

I pressed my nose against the window of the microwave, even though my dad was always saying it's not good to stand too close, and watched the bag. I concentrated on the slow *ping* of hard kernels exploding inside.

Ping . . . ping . . .

The paper bag began to puff. I waited for the popcorn. I waited for Lily. I waited to finally confess my big secret.

I hated waiting.

Now that I'd made up my mind, everything moved in slow motion. What was taking Lily so long?

Ping. The hinges of a cabinet squeaked behind me.

Lady Azura, I thought. I stared at the expanding bag. The ring of ceramic knocking ceramic harmonized with the popping corn. Dishes were being pushed about.

"Do you need help?" I asked, and turned around.

The small kitchen was empty. No Lady Azura.

The *pop, pop, pop* picked up its pace.

Two cabinet doors hung open. Doors that I was sure had been closed a minute earlier. My heartbeat quickened.

"Hello?" I called. Was Lady Azura out in the hall? "Hello?" My voice echoed.

Another cabinet opened. By itself. Just the wooden door swinging open.

My heart pounded in time with the popping kernels. I gripped the edge of the stove, fighting a sudden wave of dizziness.

A loud *click* forced me to look down by my knees. The oven's digital temperature lit up, as if it had been turned on by an invisible hand.

The oven was preheating by itself!

A white ceramic mixing bowl floated out of the cabinet and onto the island counter. A wooden spoon and a ring of silver measuring spoons flew from a drawer, clattering down next to the bowl.

Tiny electric pinpricks danced about my left foot, traveling up toward my knee. The popcorn pinged at a furious pace. I gripped the stainless-steel stove tighter.

My knuckles whitened at the pressure of my grasp. I tried desperately to control the sick feeling swirling about my stomach.

Lady Azura wasn't here.

No one alive was in this kitchen with me.

But I wasn't alone.

The popping kernels slowed their rhythm as I sucked in air. I only felt sick like this when the dead were nearby.

I squinted at the flurry of unseen activity by the counter, trying to pull a shape or the faint outline of a figure from the nothingness. Who was it? Could it be the man in the sailor cap from the blue bedroom? No, it couldn't be him—I had never seen him leave the bedroom. Maybe it was the woman who occupied the pink bedroom and cried sometimes over the loss of her baby son, Angus? No, she would have shown herself to me. We were friends. I decided it must be Henry. Mischievous little Henry, who was kept locked in a closet on the third floor. He must have gotten out and was down here to create some chaos.

I watched, transfixed, as sacks of flour and sugar floated in the air, being held by invisible arms. Too high off the ground for Henry or a child to be carrying them, I realized. Flour dust trickled from the bag's open top, leaving a white coating on the yellowed Formica as the sacks were placed on the counter. And then the dusting of flour on the counter disappeared, wiped away by invisible fingers.

"Stop it!" I hissed. Small canisters of cinnamon, nutmeg, and baking powder followed the same path from pantry to counter.

I trembled, but not because I was scared of the spirit, whoever it was. Ever since I'd come to live with Lady Azura in Stellamar, she'd been teaching me how to overcome my fear of the dead. It was this out-of-control feeling, this not knowing, that I hated.

The microwave beeped. Dry ingredients poured, as if by themselves, into the bowl.

A fork hovered above a smaller bowl that was pulled from an open cabinet. Rapidly it descended, pushing down on two peeled bananas, mashing the fruit. The scent of artificial popcorn butter mixed with a familiar tangy, overripe sweetness.

The refrigerator opened. Eggs catapulted themselves out of their side holder. Cracked shells dropped onto the counter as the bright yellow yolks plopped neatly into the large bowl. A carton of milk vibrated, as if held by an unsteady hand.

The microwave beeped again. Then the oven chimed. Alarms echoed in my head, waking me from my trance. Lily was going to be here any minute! If she walked in and I had to explain . . . I couldn't even think about where I'd begin. My plan was to ease her into the idea that I saw ghosts, not slam her with it.

I had to stop this, I realized.

I lunged toward the floating milk. I didn't spot the banana peel at my feet until I felt myself falling. Frantically, my hands reached for the island, grabbing on just as gravity almost succeed in pulling me down.

"That's it!" I cried, catching my breath. "Did you see what you almost did to me? Did you see? Show yourself!" Slowly the air before me began to shimmer. A translucent glow grew brighter and more solid. My temples throbbed with an overwhelming pressure, and the tingling ran rapidly along my leg.

My eyes widened as a plump woman with round cheeks, small dark eyes, and a bob of curly reddish hair appeared. Not quite solid like the living. Her rolled shirtsleeves revealed dimpled forearms. A ruffled white apron tied around her wide middle displayed writing in a fancy brown script. I squinted at the words: IF THEY DON'T HAVE CHOCOLATE IN HEAVEN, I'M NOT GOING.

"Funny, right?" She let out a husky laugh. "My neighbor prided herself on being the best gift giver in town. She'd start shopping in July to match the Christmas present with the person. It was a thing with her. A talent, she called it. She gave this to me one Christmas, and wouldn't you know it, that was my last Christmas." She laughed again. "A talent, for sure!"

"Who are you?" I demanded.

I'd never seen her before. Could she have stayed behind from one of Lady Azura's séances? Lady Azura had a business in our house's front room. She told fortunes and contacted clients' dead relatives.

"I'm the cook. The chef." The woman rapidly beat the batter with the wooden spoon. "The mixer of ingredients."

"You need to leave," I said. My voice wavered. What did she want? What was she doing here? I wondered.

She ignored me, scooping the mashed banana into the batter.

"This isn't your kitchen." I tried to remember all Lady Azura had taught me. *Be strong. Create boundaries. Take charge.*

"Oh, don't I know this is not my kitchen!" The woman let out another husky laugh, although this one was more of a snort. "My kitchen was state-of-the art. Really, how can one truly create in here? Ah, but we work with what we are given." She pulled a muffin pan from a lower cabinet. Her body shimmered as she moved.

"You need to leave," I tried again.

"Really, Sara, you should be more gracious, especially to a guest who cooks."

"Lady Azura!" I cried, relieved to see my great-grandmother. "She just appeared. She's taking over our kitchen!" I pointed to the spirit, now spooning batter into the muffin tin. "She needs to leave!"

"Not at all." Lady Azura waved her bony hand in the air, dismissing the idea as silly.

"But—but—" I sputtered. How could she not be concerned that a strange dead woman was cooking something in her kitchen?

"Mmmmm." Lady Azura ran her finger along the batter on the inside of the bowl, then licked her finger.

"Looks as if they're ready to bake. This part I should be able to handle."

"Good." The spirit rubbed her plump hands on her apron. "Remember, thirty minutes at three hundred fifty degrees. Check the centers with a toothpick to see that they are done."

Then she faded away completely.

My sick feeling also faded away. "What was that?"

"That was Delilah. Don't these smell divine?" She pushed the tin toward my nose.

"Yeah, great." I couldn't focus on the odor of sweet bananas and cinnamon. "You *know* her?"

"Delilah used to own the most delicious bakery in town. Delilah's Delicious Desserts, that's what it was called. The hours I'd spend there, nibbling away at her pastries . . . and Delilah was such a sweetheart." Lady Azura's thin shoulders shrugged beneath the gauzy fabric of her beige blouse. "Still is."

"Still is?" My voice sounded shrill. I didn't think I'd ever get used to how calm Lady Azura was around the dead.

"As you saw, she's stuck. Ten years gone and not alive but not yet ready to take her rightful place with the dead." Lady Azura placed the muffin tin in my hands. "All morning I couldn't stop thinking of her divine banana muffins. After all these years, I can still bring up the taste. So I summoned her."

"You just called her back from the dead?"

"Well, yes. I mean, child, you see how I burn toast"—she scrunched her angular face in disgust—"so I certainly needed help if I wanted banana muffins. Be a dear and pop these in the oven for me."

"I was sure she wanted something. That she wanted to bother us," I confessed as I slid the tin in and set the timer.

"You can't always assume the worst, Sara."

"But how am I supposed to tell if a spirit's come to do harm or to bake muffins?" I asked. "I'm serious," I added as her crimson lips turned into a thin smile.

"The only way—" The doorbell startled us. "I don't have anyone on the schedule today." Lady Azura licked her finger, then used it to smooth her flyaways. She dyed her hair a rich mahogany, but the gray roots had begun to show. At eighty-plus years old, Lady Azura still spent a lot of time on her appearance. Every morning she went through a two-hour ritual, moisturizing her skin, then applying her makeup.

I followed her through the narrow hall that led from the kitchen to the front door. Lady Azura pushed back the white curtains from the vertical window alongside the door. “It’s Beth Randazzo.”

That’s weird, I thought. *Why’s Lily’s mom here?*

I pulled open the door. Mrs. Randazzo stood alone.

“Hi!” I peered around her, across the wide porch, and down the empty sidewalk. “Where’s Lily?”

“At home. I needed her to watch Cammie and her brothers for a bit.” Mrs. Randazzo seemed jittery, which was strange. She was usually so relaxed and calm, even when her kids were causing total chaos. Now her leg bounced as she greeted Lady Azura.

“Is Mike here?” she asked as she stepped inside.

“He’s upstairs. Fixing the bathroom faucet,” Lady Azura said.

“Dad!” I bellowed. Then I turned to Mrs. Randazzo. “Why do you want to talk to my dad?”

“Something smells so good.” Mrs. Randazzo said to Lady Azura. “Bananas, is it?”

She didn’t answer my question, and she avoided looking at me. Why was she acting like this? Lily’s mom and I were close. I hung out at their house all the time. Sometimes I even pretended she was my mom too.

As my dad's sneakers made heavy thuds down the old wooden staircase, I thought back to my conversation with Mason earlier and how Mrs. Randazzo had risen from the bushes. Did this have something to do with that?

Dad greeted Lily's mom. His blue eyes crinkled at the corners as he smiled. They discussed the weather for a minute before she asked, "Is there somewhere private for us to talk?"

"Sure." Dad rubbed his hand over the light-brown stubble on his square chin. He had a thing about not shaving on the weekends. "Let's go in here." He opened the French doors leading into the front sitting room. We barely ever used this formal room. "What's it about?" he asked as she followed him toward the stiff teal sofa.

Just as the doors closed behind them, I heard her reply. My stomach dropped.

"Sara," she said. "I came to talk about Sara."

Chapter 3

I pressed my ear against the cool glass panes. Faded teal-and-gray curtains hung on the inside of the French doors, blocking my view into the room. Dad and Mrs. Randazzo spoke in low, muffled tones. I couldn't make out many of the words.

They're talking about me!

My stomach twisted. I wasn't concerned about Mrs. Randazzo telling my dad that I could see ghosts. He knew that already. It wasn't his favorite subject, but he wouldn't freak out. But what if she spilled Mason's secret? Or, even worse, what if she'd already told Lily what she'd heard? Was that the real reason why Lily wasn't here?

Lady Azura's hand gripped my shoulder. "Eavesdropping is beneath you," she scolded. "Come away."

This wasn't a request. Lady Azura never made requests. Only commands. She steered me across the hall and through the thick purple velvet curtain that covered the entrance to her rooms.

"What do you think they're saying?" I asked. "Do you know why she's here?"

"No idea," she said as we entered her fortune-telling room. Another curtain far in the back concealed her bedroom and bathroom. "But if they'd wanted you to hear, they would have invited you in."

She switched on the lamps with delicately beaded shades that were scattered about the room. Lady Azura did not believe in overhead lighting. Too harsh and unflattering, she always said. A warm yellow glow settled on the mystical room and reflected against the heavy red drapes and the red tablecloth.

"You could find out what's going on." I moved to the large, round table and peered into the crystal ball displayed on a small polished-wood pedestal. "You could see them."

"Sara, child, that is not a spy gadget. It is a tool to gaze beyond the realm of the physical eye." She dropped into her oversize armchair with the nubby dark-mustard fabric. The chair was her throne. She sat there to look into her clients' past and see their futures. She sat there when she talked to the dead.

My great-grandmother is just like me. Or I guess, I am just like her. We both talk to the dead. Lady Azura and I are the only two in our family who can. But Lady Azura can do things I can't. She can read tea leaves and tarot cards and see visions in the crystal ball. All I saw today was my reflection staring back at me. My blue eyes, usually so clear and bright, looked stormy and dark.

"Why so worried?" She tapped her long, oval nails on the arm of the chair.

I told her everything. My conversation with Mason. My suspicions about Mrs. Randazzo.

Then I hesitated. I wiggled my phone partway from the pocket of my jean shorts. I glanced quickly at the screen. No messages. Lily was being strangely quiet. She texted all the time just to say hey. Not today.

My stomach twisted tighter.

Lady Azura narrowed her brown eyes. She hated when I looked at my phone during a conversation. She said it was incredibly rude. "Finish telling me what's really bothering you. I sense there is more."

"I think I should tell Lily, if her mom hasn't beaten me to it."

"If Beth Randazzo has exposed your secret, then we'll deal with it." Lady Azura held my gaze. "But I have known Beth since she was a girl. Beth is thoughtful. I doubt she would impulsively do anything to cause you and Lily to be upset."

"You don't know that."

"True. If she has, we'll pick up the pieces. But if she hasn't told Lily, it's too soon for you to take that step."

"How can you say that?"

"I can say that because I am like you. I know. It's only been a year since you found me and we started working together. We've barely begun. You need more confidence in your abilities."

"What does that have to do with Lily knowing?"

"There are consequences to such a big reveal. You are too young to deal with them."

"You're wrong. Lily and I are both mature. We can handle it."

Lady Azura's gaze drifted to the ceiling. She twisted her arthritic hands in her lap. "Fear and disbelief bring on negativity. For years, I was labeled as crazy, because my reality did not fit with what others perceived. My sixth-grade teacher, Miss Lauria, was my favorite, most-trusted teacher. Every day I'd help her do crosswords in the school yard during lunch. We had private jokes, and she put my desk right in front of hers.

"One day I saw an intense aura about her. Dark and harmful. I confided in her. From that day on, she would no longer eat with me. She froze me out completely, refusing to call on me and moving me to the back of the classroom. I had trusted her and was devastated. I didn't understand how hurtful fear can make people."

"That won't happen with Lily."

"Are you sure?"

I remembered back to elementary school in California and the mean girls who called me "Ghost Girl." They'd whisper it as I walked through the halls. I'd hidden my abilities ever since. But Lily wasn't like those girls or Lady Azura's teacher. She wouldn't care or be scared.

Not at all.

I was pretty sure.

Almost positive.

Kind of.

"Your silence should give you pause." Lady Azura walked to the glass shelves lining the side wall. She surveyed the colorful crystals and gemstones displayed on the middle shelf. She was a big believer in the guiding energies of crystals.

She lifted a small, copper-colored crystal and brought it to me. "This is aragonite. It brings out acceptance and understanding and confidence."

She knew exactly what I needed. Acceptance from Lily. Confidence. Lots of it.

I lifted the chain from my neck. I wore all the crystals she'd given me on a necklace. Each one had a different power, and Lady Azura always seemed to give them to me at just the right time. Sometimes I couldn't figure out why she was giving me a particular one, but I had figured out a while ago that she always knew what I needed, often before I did. I threaded the reddish-brown aragonite next to my clear quartz bead and refastened the clasp. The necklace rested against my collarbone, and I could feel the slight pressure of the extra weight.

"Hi, there. What's going on?""

I turned to stare at my dad standing inside the fortune-telling room. He never came in here. Never. Fortune-telling, bringing back the dead, and all the other stuff that didn't have simple explanations made him uneasy.

"Where's Beth?" Lady Azura asked.

"Gone." He pulled one of the wooden chairs away from the table and perched awkwardly on it, watching me silently.

I squirmed under his gaze.

"Mrs. Randazzo got quite a surprise earlier today. She shared it with Lily and then . . ."

My face paled under my summer tan.

Lily knows.

Lily knows and now she's not talking to me.

"She came right over to share it with me." Dad leaned forward.

"She should've let me tell Lily," I blurted. "It wasn't how it was planned."

"You know about it?"

"Yeah." I gulped. "I figured it out when she showed up."

Lady Azura made a sympathetic *tsk-tsk* sound. This was bad. We both knew it.

"How is that possible?" Dad scratched his beard stubble. "Who told you about the lake?"

"What lake?"

"The lake the big hotel is on."

"What's a lake got to do with Lily?" Dad was usually very straightforward, but suddenly I couldn't follow him.

"Beth Randazzo came over to invite you to join them on vacation," he explained.

"Vacation at a hotel with Lily?" I asked.

"So you don't know?"

"Obviously not," Lady Azura replied with a smirk.

"Beth's sister, Angela, is a travel writer for *InTravel* magazine," Dad said.

"I know Aunt Angela," I said. Of course I did. She was Lily's favorite aunt, and she spent so much time at the house that I'd heard Lily's dad joke about charging her rent.

"Angela was assigned to write an article about a historic hotel on Lake Hoby in the Adirondack Mountains of New York, but it turns out that she didn't understand the assignment fully until today."

"What's the assignment?" Lady Azura asked.

"The magazine wants her to go undercover. They don't want the hotel to know that she's testing their claim of being the most teen-friendly hotel in the area. They want her to appear to be an ordinary guest vacationing with her teen kids, but she has no teens."

I smiled. I guessed where this was going. "I'm thirteen and so is Lily."

"Bingo! Angela wants to bring you and Lily, along with Lily's mom, to the hotel. She's going to put you to work, trying out all the activities."

I gave a loud *whoop!* Stellamar is probably more fun than most towns in the summer. It's on the beach, the ocean is warm, and the boardwalk is filled with games and rides. But if you do something over and over, even if it is playing skee-ball or jumping waves, the magic wears off. It was almost the end of the summer, and I was ready to leave the Jersey shore for a new adventure in the mountains.

"I take it that means you want to go," Dad teased. "Mrs. Randazzo came to clear it with me before Lily told you."

"And that's all she had to talk about?"

"What else is there?"

I glanced at Lady Azura and shrugged. "Nothing. Nothing at all."

Lady Azura gave a satisfied nod, and the wrinkles along the corners of her lips deepened as she gave a slight smile. She was happy that Lily didn't know. I was happy for a different reason. I wanted to be the one to tell her. It was my secret to share when I chose to share it.

"Something's buzzing out there." Dad leaned his head toward the hall.

"Oh, my muffins!" Lady Azura scurried toward the kitchen. She didn't move very fast. She had arthritis in her hips and couldn't climb the steep stairs to the second and third floors where Dad and I lived in the old Victorian house we shared. "I hope they don't burn. Delilah will be so disappointed."

Relief flooded over me. I needed a break from this house and all its supernatural energy.

I glanced down at the screen of my phone. Texts poured in from Lily. Her mom must've told her the trip was a go.

WE GET 2 SHARE A ROOM!! U & ME 2GETHER ON VACA!!!!!!!

!!!!!!!!! I texted back.

Then it dawned on me. The two of us together in a hotel room. Away from everyone in Stellamar. Best friends swimming during the day and sharing secrets at night in the dark. What better place to tell her?

"Are you sure you want to go?" Dad asked. "You don't have to leave—"

"Are you kidding? I can't wait!"

"Oh, well, yeah, I can see that." Dad's face fell. "I guess I haven't been that fun, working all the time. It's just that, kiddo, we've never been apart. You know?"

Dad was right. Since I was born and Mom died giving birth to me, it'd always been just the two of us. We were a pair, a team, the "dynamic duo," Dad called us. We didn't go on a lot of vacations, but when we did, it'd always been together.

Until now.

I felt bad. "Will you be okay? It's only for five days, right?"

"Right." He brightened. "I'm being silly. It's supposed to be the kid who doesn't want to leave the parent, not the other way around."

"We can ease into it," I suggested. "Practice this week like we did when I didn't want to go to pre-school. Remember how we'd do pretend drop-offs at the school the week before?"

"Ah, you're good to me, kiddo, but I'm going have to rip the Band-Aid off quickly. There's no time for practicing."

"Really? When am I going?"

"Your vacation starts tomorrow."

Chapter 4

The air smelled different. Clearer. Crisper. The saltiness and humidity of the shore had been replaced by pine sap and a cool breeze. I leaned my head out the car window, letting my hair flutter behind as I inhaled.

"How much longer?" Lily asked. She pushed the empty cheese-puff bag and candy wrappers from the backseat onto the floor. We'd been driving north for over four hours.

"Minutes," Mrs. Randazzo said, glancing at the GPS screen. "We just need to follow the curve of the lake."

Outside my window, a water-skier cut a wake through the deep blue waters of Lake Hoby.

"Okay, time for a quick recap," Aunt Angela announced from the passenger seat. "Our story isn't too far from the truth. I'm taking my sister, my niece, and her friend on vacation. No one needs to know I'm writing an article or the name of the magazine. We'll have fun, experience everything, and that's that."

"Works for me," Lily said, twirling her hair around her finger. Her mom and aunt had the same dark, shiny hair, but Angela had recently cut hers into a short, shaggy haircut that looked amazing on her. Lily had considered getting the same haircut for about a day but then decided she couldn't part with her long waves of hair. I'd probably never have the guts to get a haircut like that. I tugged at my own blond ponytail as if to make sure it was still there.

"Here's the lowdown on the hotel." Angela propped her bare feet on the dashboard and crossed her tanned legs. Her toenails were painted pale pink, and she wore white shorts with a really pretty gauzy floral shirt. Piles of thin bangle bracelets jangled on each arm. Her outfit was so simple, but it looked great on her. Lily was like that too—she could make anything look fantastic. She must get it from her aunt. Lady Azura would probably call it "having real style."

"The house was built in 1910 by the wealthy Helliman family as a summer retreat from the city. Mr. Helliman owned the biggest soap company in the nation. Mega money, we're talking."

Angela swiveled so she could better see Lily and me. "In 1924 a fire destroyed a large portion of the house. In the 1940s, the house was purchased by someone else and turned into a hotel named Helliman House. The hotel did well for years. This area has always been a big summer getaway spot. But the owner didn't keep things up, and the hotel got shabby. Really gross, I hear."

"You're taking us to a run-down hotel?" Lily sounded horrified.

"Of course not!" Angela laughed and snapped her gum, a gesture that reminded me of Lily. "This other guy, Grant Himoff, bought Helliman House about five years ago. Got it for a steal, I hear. He did major renovations. Top-notch. He's trying to attract families with waterslides, boating, and game rooms."

She trained her gaze on us. "The key is that this Mr. Himoff cannot know what I'm really up to. I'm trusting that you girls can keep a secret."

Could I keep a secret? Bring it on! My list of secrets grew longer and longer every day.

"Up ahead!" Mrs. Randazzo called from the driver's seat.

Lily and I craned our necks, searching the few gaps in the sky-high pine trees that lined the winding road and cast the car in shadow.

Then a huge hotel appeared in a clearing before us.

White clapboard gleamed in the brilliant afternoon sun. Hunter-green shutters sandwiched the numerous windows running the enormous length of the three-story building. A large deck extended along the front. Dark-green Adirondack chairs were angled for the best views of the majestic mountains.

We drove up a circular drive. The front section of the hotel, though updated, was older, and the additions, which arched out from either side to form a horseshoe toward the back of the property, had been added more recently. Guests played croquet on the wide front lawn.

"Welcome to Helliman House!" Two cute college-age guys dressed in white polo shirts and white pants greeted us as we tumbled out of the car.

"Hello, hello!" Angela chirped, settling her oversize cat's-eye sunglasses over her eyes. "We're checking in. Staying for five glorious days!"

Even though it was for Angela's job, she and Lily's

mom were giddy about their getaway. They had left all the little kids with the dads.

The blond guy opened the trunk to take our bags and tipped his head in surprise. Lily, Mrs. Randazzo, and I had each packed a small duffel. Angela traveled with five large matching hot-pink leather bags. I couldn't guess what she was doing with all those clothes for five days in the mountains. That must come with the territory of being so stylish.

Lily and I entered the lobby right behind her mom and aunt. A rustic wood reception desk lined one side, directly across from a magnificent old stone fireplace. Knotty pine furniture, clustered in intimate groupings, filled the room.

"Check that out." Lily pointed out the windows along the back wall. A sloping green lawn dotted with white Adirondack chairs led down to a large pool with a towering waterslide. Beyond the pool lay a small marina with colorful sailboats, paddleboards, and shiny motorboats. Lake Hoby shimmered in the afternoon sun.

"Mom, can we go to the lake?" Lily asked.

"In a sec." Mrs. Randazzo and Aunt Angela were

giving the young girl behind the desk, who wore a name tag that said SOFIA—HERE TO HELP, information to check into our rooms.

Sofia was very peppy, asking Angela questions and handing her packets of information on hotel activities. Her mane of strawberry-blond curls bounced as she talked. "So you have two adjoining rooms. Shall I get separate card keys for all four of you?"

"Definitely!" Lily said. We wanted to be able to explore on our own.

"The hotel is so large," her mom commented, staring at an illustrated map. "Where are we staying?"

"Let's see." Sofia glanced at her computer. "Oh"—her perky smile vanished for a second, but she quickly composed herself—"you're in the main building on the second floor."

Angela noticed Sofia's falter. "Is that bad?"

"Not at all. That's the historic part. The original house. It's supernice. It was just redone." Sofia glanced over her shoulder. A door to her left labeled PRIVATE was slightly ajar. She leaned over the desk toward us. "Some people say the second floor is . . . haunted."

"Haunted?" Lily squealed. "Really?"

Taking Lily's broad smile as encouragement, Sofia nodded. "That's the rumor. I think it's so cool, don't you? I've never seen anything, but if I were staying in an old hotel, I'd want it to have ghosts."

I didn't think it was cool. I'd just left one haunted house, and now I was checking into another?

My eyes darted about the lobby. Framed black-and-white photos of people in old-fashioned clothing lined the walls. Several guests, some in tennis clothes, milled about. Everyone seemed solid and alive. I had no weird tingly feelings. The air felt vibrant and happy.

Sofia's wrong, I thought. *Just because this place is old doesn't mean it's haunted.*

"Sara." Mrs. Randazzo placed her hand gently on my arm. "If you want, we can get a different room."

Had my face betrayed my fear? Or was she remembering the conversation I was still hoping she hadn't overheard?

"You look a bit pale," she said quietly.

"No, no, I'm fine," I insisted. "It's the long drive, that's all."

"Sara's not afraid of a haunted hotel room, are you, Sara?" Lily clapped her hands together the way she always did when she was excited. "I'll keep you safe from the supernatural. We'll be ghost gathers together!"

I didn't know what a ghost gather was, but I decided not to ask. Better just to nod and smile.

"Haunted how?" Angela pressed Sofia. "What do guests report? Noises? Sightings of actual ghosts?"

The PRIVATE door swung open, and a broad-shouldered man in a pressed navy blazer and green tie moved quickly beside Sofia. "Hello, hello, Grant Himoff here. I want to personally welcome you." He shook Aunt Angela's hand, then Mrs. Randazzo's. "Sofia just started with us. Summer job, right, Sofia? Just out of high school. So young."

All smiles, he waved over one of the front-door guys. "Spencer, please show these beautiful ladies to their rooms. I'm sure they want to start their vacations. Complimentary smoothies are being served for the next hour down by the pool."

In a flash, Spencer, the blond guy in all white from out front, corralled us out of the lobby and down a short hall leading to the elevators.

I glanced back. Mr. Himoff bent his head toward Sofia, talking rapidly in a low tone, probably lecturing her about scaring guests with ghost stories.

The elevator let us off on the second floor. Hallways, wallpapered in a green-and-beige stripe, stretched to the left and right. Lily shifted her sequined tote bag onto her shoulder and headed right.

"Whoa! Wrong way," Spencer called.

Lily pivoted and followed him, her mom, and aunt to the left, but I lingered, staring down the wrong hall. Something felt odd in that direction.

Quieter. Dimmer.

The light fixtures, designed to resemble candles, were all dark down the right hall but burned bright down the left.

"Why are there no lights here?" I called out.

"That wing isn't in use right now." Spencer kept walking.

"Why not?" Aunt Angela asked.

"Renovations." Spencer shrugged. "They aren't using any of those rooms while they fix them up. Off-limits. Here you go."

Spencer opened the doors to our rooms.

"I call the bed by the window!" Lily flung herself across the green sateen bedspread. "Are you good there?"

I perched on the second bed, close to the bathroom but directly across from a large flat-screen TV.

"Sure thing, but I control the remote." I clicked on a cooking show, just to tease Lily. She hated watching people cook.

"We'll see about that!" She lunged to grab the remote from my hand, but I was too quick. I snatched a pillow and bopped her on the head.

Giggling, she reached for my second pillow and whacked me back.

"Girls!" Mrs. Randazzo called. "Stop acting like savages. What's poor Spencer here going to think?"

I stole a glance at Spencer. He smiled. He had no problem with a pillow fight.

Angela thrust glossy, printed sheets of activities into our hands. "Look at all the fun stuff they have for kids your age. Throw on suits while we unpack." She glanced through the door leading to their room. Her pink luggage teetered in a pile. She seemed to have suddenly realized just how much she'd brought with her. "It's going to take me a little while to unpack. We'll meet you down at the pool."

"Let's go claim some lounge chairs," Lily suggested.

Mrs. Randazzo made us listen to a long list of rules. We couldn't swim without a lifeguard. We couldn't leave the hotel property. We had to stay together. She went on and on. Finally, Mrs. Randazzo and Angela retreated to their room. I pulled on my favorite aqua-and-navy halter one-piece. Lily slipped into her magenta ruffled bikini. We both threw on the matching paisley tunics we'd bought together last month at a stand on the boardwalk and hurried back to the elevator.

"What am I missing?" Lily rummaged through her bag as we waited for the elevator to open. "I got sunscreen, lip balm, floppy hat, sunglasses, cards, celebrity magazines. . . ."

My attention drifted down the darkened hallway. The hallway that was off-limits.

Dim light filtered in from a small window at the far end. Shadows swirled about in the silence. My shoulders stiffened as my eyes caught a shape moving.

I squinted, trying desperately to see. A figure. Small. A long skirt or a robe formed a triangle by her feet. A ropelike braid fell down her back.

I blinked rapidly. Was Sofia right? Was this floor haunted?

"Who's that?" Lily hissed.

Lily saw her too. What did *that* mean?

"Hello? Hello, down there!" Lily called.

Her voiced echoed back. The hall was now empty. All we heard was the faint *click* of a guest room door shutting.

And the chime of the elevator as the door opened.

Lily looked wide-eyed at me. I looked at her. We both hurried into the elevator.

In the lobby, Lily grabbed my hand. "We need to report this."

"Report what?" I wasn't sure what we'd seen.

"Mr. Himoff!" Lily barreled toward the reception desk. She was an act-first, think-later girl. I liked to turn things over in my mind, but today Lily was leading the show. "We just saw the weirdest thing."

Mr. Himoff kept his usual broad smile but cautioned Lily to lower her voice. He nodded at a group of guests in the lobby preparing to set out for a hike up Mount Norma.

Lily told him and Sofia, who stood by his side, about our strange sighting.

"That's impossible," he scoffed. "That hall is being

renovated. No one is staying in those rooms."

Lily insisted we'd seen a woman.

"Must've been a cleaning woman." He didn't seem overly concerned, but he promised to send security people to check it out.

"Ah, Mrs. Foster and Darius!" he turned his back on us to greet a woman and her young son. "What can I do for you?"

Sofia waved us to the far side of the desk. "That hallway," she whispered, "the one he said is closed for renovations. That's not the truth. It's closed because that's where the ghosts are."

"Sofia!" Mr. Himoff's voice boomed in the high-ceiled lobby. "Darius here is looking for a checkers set."

Sofia gave us a grim smile and went to help Darius. Lily and I took off out the back doors and across the sloping lawn.

"Do you think we saw a ghost?" Lily asked. Her voice was filled with wonder.

"I don't know." I didn't, really.

"That would be so amazing if we did. Can you imagine?"

I could.

Lily stopped as we reached the white fence circling the pool. "We need to go back. To explore. Tonight, okay?"

"Okay." My mind jolted with sudden possibilities.

Lily clapped her hands together. "What if we find a ghost?"

This was it. The perfect intro. I couldn't have scripted it better. *If we find a ghost, I can talk with it because that's what I do. . . .* I formulated the words in my brain.

Here we go, I thought.

"If we find—"

"Hi." Lily's voice came out low and giggly. "You taking tickets or something?"

Two boys about our age leaned against the fence, blocking our way in.

"Just name, rank, and fingerprints," said the taller of the two. He flipped his long brown bangs off his forehead and narrowed his hazel eyes.

"So this is your job? Pool police?" Lily asked, grinning.

"Waterslide warrior, at your service." The boy crossed his arms in a tough-guy pose. His biceps were more muscular than most guys I knew. "This is my sidekick." He nodded toward the skinny boy at his side with a mop of dark curls. "He specializes in wet towels."

"I do not, Wyatt!" The mop-haired boy blushed, then swatted his friend with, of all things, a wet towel. "And I'm not your sidekick."

"Owen's a little sensitive. I keep whupping him in waterslide races." He turned to the slides towering above the pool. Two tubes twirled downward, spitting out swimmers side by side into the deep end.

"You up for it?" Wyatt asked Lily. "Me against you?"

Lily's eyes shone. She never backed down from a challenge. "Bring it!"

I watched as she dropped her bag on an empty chaise lounge, peeled off her tunic and kicked off her sandals, then confidently followed Wyatt to the slide.

Owen stood silently next to me, twisting the towel in his hands.

So much for telling Lily, I thought. The perfect opportunity—and now it was gone.

I turned to Owen. "Want to swim?"

Chapter 5

"I went down the slide twenty-five times," Lily reported to her mom and Aunt Angela that night at dinner. "And then we floated in chair rafts while we drank strawberry-banana smoothies in the pool."

"So Helliman House is getting a thumbs-up so far?" Angela inquired.

"Totally," I said. "And we haven't even hit the lake yet."

Lily speared a crouton from her Caesar salad as she scanned the main room of the restaurant. I knew she was looking for Wyatt. While we were getting dressed for dinner, she'd talked of nothing else. Wyatt was fourteen and from New York City. He went to a fancy private school, rode the subway all by himself, and had just finished a summer at an all-boys summer camp. Lily thought he was very sophisticated. And cute.

Very cute.

Owen, it turned out, had just met Wyatt here yesterday. His family was from some town near Chicago. He hadn't talked much, but when he did, he had a sort of sarcastic sense of humor that I kind of liked.

"Sara, look!" Lily grabbed my shoulder. "It's her!"

"Who?" Mrs. Randazzo asked.

Neither Lily nor I answered. We stared at the woman being shown by the hostess to the table next to us. She wore a simple sundress, and her auburn hair was twisted in a long, loose braid she'd swooped over her shoulder. Dozens of woven hemp bracelets covered both wrists.

"You're right," I whispered.

"She's not a ghost." Lily sounded disappointed.

"Okay, spill it," Angela said, her eyes sparkling. "What're we talking about?"

In low tones, we told Angela about the hallway and how Sofia said renovations weren't being done there because it was possibly haunted.

"Interesting." Angela glanced at the woman sitting alone at the table, reading the menu. "Maybe there's a story here." She leaned her chair back, nearly tipping, and called, "Eating alone?"

The woman raised her menu as if to protect herself, but then smiled shyly when she saw Lily's grinning aunt. "Yes."

"You must join us. We're just starting, and more is merrier!" Angela waved the woman over to our table.

The woman looked unsure.

"Angie," Lily's mom said under her breath, "some people go on vacation to be *alone*."

"I'm Angela Fiorini." Angela ignored her older sister and extended her arm, still stacked with bracelets, but I noticed that she seemed to have changed them to match her outfit.

The slight woman pushed her chair next to Angela's. "Laura L'Angille. I will join you, thanks." Her voice was high, almost childlike.

We filled Laura in on who we were, but we kept Angela's secret. No talk of being a reporter.

Laura came from Tupper Lake, which wasn't far from the hotel. She was into yoga and meditation, and she loved the outdoors. Oddly, she and Angela discovered a lot to talk about. They were a funny pair. Angela in her stylish maxi-dress and delicate gold sandals and Laura in her crunchy fabric sandals and woven jewelry.

"Vacationing so close to home?" Angela asked. She was good at getting information.

"I'm here for work," Laura explained.

"Oh, a conference. This is a great spot for one," Mrs. Randazzo remarked.

"Not exactly. They don't have conferences for what I do," Laura said. "I'm a spiritual adviser."

Laura explained that she combined herbal and spiritual practices to balance the body, mind, and spirit. She was concerned with inner peace and harmony. She hadn't had her business long, but she felt she was developing a following in the area.

Lily was delighted by her tales of healing people by using her psychic abilities to unearth their hidden troubles. I hung back, not trusting myself to say anything. Not trusting Laura.

Angela had stopped acting like a reporter and, by the time we finished sharing a gooey chocolate lava cake, was comparing favorite recipes with Laura. "Come to the Bearside with me and Beth," she invited her. The Bearside was an adults-only pub on the hotel's lower level. Lily and I had already announced that we were heading to the game room.

"I wish I could, but I have to work," Laura said.

"Work?" Angela raised her eyebrows.

"On the second floor," Lily blurted. "You're communicating with the ghosts on the second floor, right?"

"Mr. Himoff hired me." She lowered her voice, and we all huddled close. "He's having a problem with—"

"Ghosts!" Lily finished.

"Shhhhh," Laura cautioned. "He doesn't want people to know. I shouldn't have said anything."

"Come on," Angela encouraged. "Spill the dirt. I love a good story."

"Ever since he bought the hotel, guests staying in the rooms on one hallway have complained about hearing odd, mournful noises. There have been reports of the heat mysteriously turning on in the night and doors refusing to lock." Laura glimpsed over her shoulder. No one seemed to be listening. "Things got so bad he had to comp the complaining guests."

"Comp? What's that?" I asked.

"It means he gave them a night's stay complimentary. Free," Mrs. Randazzo explained.

"One free night is no big deal. But he's had to give a lot, especially to stop the guests from posting bad reviews online. Lots of free nights means losing lots of money," Laura said.

"How do you figure in?" Angela asked.

"Mr. Himoff closed off the hallway several weeks ago, but he wants to use the rooms again, so I'm here to clear the negative energy."

"How do you know it's ghosts?" I asked. "Couldn't the heating be wacky and the doors not work?"

"The building stuff has been checked by experts. Nothing is physically wrong." Laura folded her hands. "Just spiritually. I'm here to encourage them to move on."

"I don't think that's fair," Lily said.

"Fair?" All the adults faced Lily.

"Yeah, how is it fair to force the ghosts from their home? I mean, what gives you or Mr. Himoff the right to kick them out?" Lily demanded.

"I like how you think," Laura said. "It's a tricky question, but in this case, Mr. Himoff owns the building, and I've been hired to do a job."

"Do you think you can do it?" Lily's mom asked.

Exactly what I was wondering. I wasn't getting any psychic vibe from Laura, but then again, I'd never guessed Mason had powers until he told me.

So maybe that's not my thing.

"Yes." Laura sounded confident. "I'm sure I can."

"Except for the weirdness down the hall, Helliman House is amazing," I said as we entered the game room. The walls were a glossy dark green, and low white leather sofas were gathered around tables that looked like tree stumps. One wall was lined with every video game imaginable. A pool table, Ping-Pong table, air hockey table, and a huge screen projecting a dance simulation game took up the rest of the space. Along the far wall, a bar with neon lights served sodas and fruity drinks with crazy straws.

"I think the ghosts down the hall make this place even better," Lily said. "Laura's great. She's so serene, not freaky like you'd expect a spiritual adviser to be."

"Lady Azura's not freaky," I countered.

"Seriously?" Lily laughed.

I joined in. "Okay, but freaky good."

"True," Lily agreed.

I hoped she'd think I was freaky good too, when I told her.

"Are you girls better at this kind of pool than the

swimming pool?" Wyatt called from the pool table.

"I demolished you on that waterslide," Lily countered.

"The girl's delusional." Wyatt turned to Owen and a tall girl with a shaggy pixie cut and dark-mascara lashes. Both held pool cues.

"Owen, back me up here. Did I not win today?" Lily's face broke into a flirtatious smile.

"I have to say, man, you were looking a little slow on the descent." Owen lined up the white ball and knocked the solid red ball into the far corner pocket.

"Wyatt has water on his brain," the girl remarked. "Always has. Did you know he wore arm floaties until he was eight?"

"Don't listen to Kayla." Wyatt elbowed her. "She's just jealous. She can't hit the ball to save her life."

Kayla playfully poked his side with her cue. "You talk a good game, yet Owen is destroying you."

"Just warming up till Lily and Sara arrived." He passed pool cues to us. "They can be on my team. These girls are so tight. They never part."

"It's a best friend thing," Lily explained.

As we racked up the balls and began to play, Kayla

and Wyatt continued their competitive banter. Neither Lily nor I were sure who Kayla was or how she fit in. After a while, Lily asked, “How do you guys know each other?”

“We met long, long ago in Central Park when we were five.” Kayla had a very dramatic way of speaking. “We’ve been together for the good, bad, and ugly ever since.”

“Together?” Lily repeated.

“Eww! No, not that kind of together.” Kayla flung her willowy arms. “Our nannies were pals. We played together and we used to go to the same school, and now our families vacation together.”

“You go to different schools now?” I asked.

“I go to Cleveland, do you know it? It’s a private school in the city for performing. You have to audition to get in.” Kayla jutted out her hip. “It’s a good thing, because I’m never there and they’re cool about it. They let you miss class if you’re in a show.”

“Show?” Lily loved to sing and dance. “You’re in a show in New York City?”

“I was in *We Are All Trees*. It ran off-Broadway.” Kayla was enjoying Lily’s attention.

"Off-off," Wyatt echoed. "Way off."

Owen grunted, not looking up from the table. He seemed intent on calculating the perfect angle.

"You were on *Broadway*?" Lily had stars in her eyes.

Lily and Kayla stopped playing, so Kayla could tell her all about her theater glory.

I hovered between them and the table. Owen was on a roll, dropping one ball, then the other into the pockets as Wyatt groaned. Neither pair paid attention to me.

I watched Kayla dazzle Lily. "Hey, Lil," I began, creating an excuse to drag Lily away. "We promised your mom we'd only stay for—"

I stopped myself. I know I was sometimes too quick to judge people. Kayla hadn't done anything bad, I reminded myself.

My phone buzzed. Mason. I glanced at his text. DO IT YET?

I sighed. It hadn't been so easy to get Lily alone.

SOON, I texted back.

An hour later, Lily scooped her arm through mine, and we headed up to our room.

"Laura!" Lily called as the elevator door opened

onto our floor. The air had a sweet, earthy smell. "What're you doing?"

Laura stood midway down the darkened not-in-use hallway. She waved a bunch of tiny dried sticks. "Quiet," she warned, motioning us over. "I'm not supposed to attract attention from the guests." She moved her bundle of sticks around the door frame of room 24. "I'm smudging."

"Smudging?" I wasn't sure I'd heard right.

"Smudging lines up the energy of a space. Makes the positive outweigh the negative."

"How do you do that?" Lily asked.

"This is white sage. It's an herb." She held up the bundle of twigs with dried silvery-green leaves. "I light the sage. Then I walk from room to room with the smoking sage and chant. That's smudging. Like a housecleaning for spirits. Join me."

Lily followed Laura to the next door. I started, then stopped.

A maid stood in my way.

She wore the crisp, green cotton Helliman House maid uniform. Her dark hair circled her wide cheeks in a chin-length bob. The skin under her eyes was puffy, and her shoulders slumped with exhaustion. She carried a set of fresh sheets in her arms.

Arms that shimmered.

Arms barely visible.

The tingling started in my foot.

I swallowed hard. The maid wasn't alive.

A purple plastic watch that all the department stores advertised last year circled her wrist. The maid hadn't died that long ago if she was wearing that watch.

I glanced at Laura and Lily, still busy waving sage. Was this the ghost Laura was smudging out?

The maid headed toward them. Another pain shot through my chest, and I knew. The maid had died from a heart attack.

Had something here caused her heart to stop?

"It's working," Laura whispered suddenly. "There's a presence."

Lily froze. I watched Laura closely. She knew the maid was here!

"With the heat of this fire, I purify this space." Laura raised the smoking sage and chanted. "Be gone, be gone, be gone."

And she was.

I blinked. The maid had disappeared. Totally gone.

Laura inhaled deeply. "The spirit has moved on."

"Really?" Lily cried. "You saw a ghost? And then you saw it leave?"

"I have heightened senses, so I feel them. I feel their energy, and I can feel it move on," Laura explained. "No one actually sees the dead."

Not true, I thought. But I wasn't going there. Not yet.

Suddenly I had new respect for Laura. She wasn't a fake.

"So that's it?" Lily asked. "Ghost gone?"

"Hard to say." Lily reached into a canvas tote at her feet and pulled out two more sage bundles. "Let's cover the hall together. Then I'll move onto the second level of cleansing myself."

Stepping up to room 22 across the hall, I raised the herbs. I was itching to call Lady Azura and fill her in on smudging. Did she know about it? It seemed so much easier to smoke out a spirit than all the work Lady Azura did with séances.

"It's not a song, Lily," Laura said, correcting her melodic *"Be gone, be gone."* "To get rid of the negative, focus inward and let your intention out as you chant."

I did as Laura instructed and how Lady Azura had taught me. Closing my eyes, I blocked the sound of Laura and Lily's chants and pulled into myself. The energy swirling about settled itself in me. My body felt weightless.

Then a burst of heat. Hot, thick air blanketed my face.

My eyes opened to a wall of orange-yellow flames.

Flames crackled and danced inches before me.

A wail rose from the fire. A cry of pain. Someone was trapped in there. In the fire. A girl screaming.

Lily? Was it Lily screaming?

"Lily!" I cried.

"Shhh, Sara. We don't want to get Laura in trouble."

Lily stood beside me, eyes bright with adventure. She pirouetted, then pretended the sage was a bouquet of flowers she'd caught onstage. She giggled her familiar lilting laugh.

I stared at the closed door to room 22. No fire. No flames.

What had just happened?

Laura appeared by my side. She stared at the door, as if seeing through it, and her body stiffened. Her hand reached for the doorknob, then pulled back.

"Time for bed," she announced suddenly. Her smiled was forced. She'd felt something. Someone.

Lily and I protested, but Laura insisted, "It's late. We're done here for the night."

She ushered us to our room and handed us over to Lily's mom, who was already in her nightgown.

Later, after Lily and I were both tucked into our beds and the adjoining door to her mom's room was closed, Lily got up and flicked on the bathroom light. "You won't tell Miranda or Avery?"

"Of course not," I promised. I was the only one of our friends who knew Lily was still afraid of the dark. I liked that she trusted me.

Lily slipped back under her covers. "What happened back there? One minute Laura was all 'let's smudge together,' and then she couldn't get us away fast enough."

"I know." I didn't tell Lily about my vision, if that's what it was. It happened so fast. Maybe I made it up.

"Laura sensed something behind that door. I saw it in her face." Lily sat straight and slapped her hand over her mouth. "Sara, there's a ghost in room twenty-two!"

Chapter 6

"It's our ghost. We were there when Laura discovered it," Lily explained the next morning while we water-skied with her mom and Angela. "If we tell Aunt Angela, she'll poke around. She's got that reporter's mind, and she questions everything. She'll probably want to try and disprove it. We need to check it out first."

I didn't want to search out ghosts, but I agreed. I was scared of the info Mrs. Randazzo might spill about me if we told.

"You won't believe what happened after we left you guys last night," Lily confided to Wyatt, Owen, and Kayla after we'd hooked up with the Teen Club for an afternoon hike up Mount Norma. I was surprised she was telling them. What happened to "our ghost"?

Pushing a tree branch aside to follow the narrow,

rocky path leading up the mountain, I listened as Lily dramatically recounted Laura's reaction. She didn't know the half of it—the maid or the flames—but our new friends were fascinated with the possibility of a ghost in room 22.

"Lily, we so have to go check it out!" Kayla gushed. She'd dressed for the role of hiker in khaki shorts, a cute denim shirt, and hiking boots. I'd just thrown on cutoffs, a purple tank, and my gray sneakers. I wondered if Kayla had a costume for every activity.

"A ghost-hunting trip," Wyatt said.

We hung back from the group leader, who gathered the other teens under a cluster of pines for a water break.

"Ghosts aren't real," Owen scoffed as he bent to examine another rock. He was looking for tiny fossils in the sandstones. Trilobites, he called them. He had a collection at home.

"You don't know that," Lily countered.

"Do you have any proof?" Owen asked. "In science, it rests on you to prove it, more than I need to disprove it."

"Fine, Mr. Scientist," Kayla said. "We'll prove it. We'll all go to the room after we get down from here."

"You can't," I said. "The hall is off-limits."

"Is it blocked?" Wyatt asked.

"Is there a sign or that yellow tape warning people away?" Kayla asked, teaming up with Wyatt.

"No," I admitted. I shot Lily a meaningful stare.

She met my gaze, looking suddenly unsure. Was she wishing she'd kept this just between us? "We could get in trouble," she said.

"Are you chicken?" Wyatt challenged Lily.

"Me? Please." Lily rolled her eyes.

"Then you're in?" he asked. "Room twenty-two?"

"All the way." Kayla scooted over a tree root and wrapped her arm around Lily's shoulder. "Aren't we, Lil?"

"Sure." Lily looked over at me. "Good, Sara?"

"Good," I agreed, even though I knew it was a bad idea.

A very bad idea.

We ditched the frozen lemonade cooldown in the teen activity center and took the elevator to the second floor.

"This is dumb," Owen muttered as we filed silently down the dim hallway.

"I'm with you on that," I said quietly.

"Yeah?" He seemed pleased.

"Locked, locked, locked." Wyatt rattled the knob on each door. We stood in a semicircle around the door to room 22.

"This is it?" Kayla asked. "I don't feel anything."

"Yes." Lily grabbed the knob and twisted. "Not that it matters, since everything is locked. Maybe we should—" The door pushed open.

For a moment, we all stared in surprise. A hotel room similar to mine and Lily's lay silently before us. Two queen beds with matching green bedspreads, a desk, a TV, an armchair, and a window looking out onto the lake. Nothing special.

Kayla entered and we all followed.

Wyatt bounced on a bed. "Scoot over, ghost!"

"Yoo-hoo, anyone home?" Kayla peeked behind the heavy curtains. "Come out, come out, wherever you are!"

"That's not how Laura did it," Lily said. "We need to be calmer."

"Oh, like yoga. I take a yoga class in the city with Avani Patel. Do you know her? She meditates with all the big-name stars." Kayla sat cross-legged on the floor and folded her hands by her heart.

Lily dropped down beside her.

Owen perched on the desk, but I stayed rooted in the center of the room. The pins-and-needles feeling had started in my foot.

I knew this was a bad idea.

"There's nothing here." My voice sounded more confident than I felt. "Let's take a canoe out. Lil, we never got to do that yesterday."

"Not now, Sara. Meditate with us." She followed Kayla in a series of forced breaths.

"Omm . . . om . . . ," Owen teased.

Lily giggled until Kayla shushed her.

"Ghost, oh, ghost! Show yourself!" Wyatt commanded.

My entire body prickled with an itchy heat. I scratched my neck. Then I saw her.

Waist-length red hair falling in loose waves.

Long, white cotton nightgown. Ruffles around the wrists and collar. Nothing a girl today would sleep in.

But she wasn't from today.

She wasn't even alive.

Her body had that shimmery, real-but-not-real quality I'd seen many times before.

She looked about sixteen. Her slender bare feet poked out from beneath the nightgown.

Wyatt continued to make jokes, calling for the ghost.

He had no idea she stood right here.

No one did. Except me.

Ghost girl reached out and placed her translucent hand on Lily's dark hair.

Lily's shoulders stiffened.

Had she felt something?

The ghost girl stroked Lily's hair, as if petting her. Her dark eyes had no pupils, and she focused them on my best friend.

Lily squirmed and tucked a strand of hair behind her ears.

Ghost girl crouched down. Closer to Lily. She ran her fingers down Lily's bare arm.

Goose bumps sprang up, and with a slight shiver, Lily hugged her arms about her.

Ghost girl moved in closer. Nearly on top of her.

Closer. Closer.

What was she doing to Lily? I reached out to push her away.

A wave of hot air rushed over me as my hand connected with the spirit.

The ghost girl began to glow. A halo of orange light shone from around her body.

I squinted and pulled back. I'd never seen this before.

The air turned thick and suffocating. I gulped, desperate to wet my dry throat. My head throbbed. All I could see was the glow of orange.

Brilliant orange light.

And then the red-haired girl came back into focus.

No Lily. No Kayla. No hotel.

The red-haired girl sat on a large four-poster bed. Pale pink canopy. Ivory wallpaper with tiny pink flowers. A window with white curtains let in the humidity of a summer rain and the scent of lavender. The lake glimmered in the distance.

Another girl in a white nightgown sat beside her on the bed. Her face stayed hidden under a curtain of dark hair that the red-haired girl brushed with a silver-backed brush.

"Make my bed and light the light." The dark-haired girl's voice rang out clear and high.

"I'll be home tonight," sang the red-haired girl.

"Blackbird, bye-bye." They finished the verse together with a failed try at harmony.

The dark-haired girl, her body smaller and narrower, bent over and let out a giggle. A deep, infectious giggle that caused the red-haired girl to smile.

The giggle grew louder.

The room grew hotter.

My skin burned. Laughter rang in my ears.

"What're you doing? Why are you here?"

I sucked in my breath. She was talking to me!

Chapter 7

The voice had come from Laura. She stood in the doorway, her body rigid, her eyes angry slits.

The bed and the pretty floral room were gone. So was the dark-haired girl.

The red-haired spirit remained. Next to Lily.

Wyatt motioned to Owen, and the two boys dodged around Laura and out the door. Cowards.

"We just—" Lily began to explain.

Laura held up her hand and moved toward Lily. We watched as she turned both palms skyward. "There's an energy here. A strong energy."

"A ghost? There's a ghost?" Lily asked. She stood. There were only inches between her and the spirit.

Laura nodded. I remained frozen.

"Oh, please, I don't feel any ghost," Kayla scoffed.

"I do," Lily said quietly. "I think."

“Seriously?” Kayla widened her eyes.

“Who are you?” Laura asked.

“Kayla Graham.”

“Well, Kayla, if you are going to be here”—Laura gave each of us a pointed look—“although none of you should be here, I need you to be quiet and contain your negative energy.”

Kayla opened her mouth to respond, then closed it. She’d noticed Lily was captivated by Laura.

The red-haired girl’s eerie gaze remained fixed on Lily. She didn’t care about Kayla or Laura—or me.

But I could feel her.

Her heat.

Her energy.

Angry. Negative.

Much more negative than anything Kayla threw off.

“She’s lost,” Laura said quietly. Her eyes fluttered closed. “She wants to go home.”

“Where’s home?” Lily turned, squaring her body with the spirit’s shimmery form.

The ghost girl bent to grasp Lily’s hand. I jolted from my stupor and yanked Lily’s other hand.

"We need to go," I announced. My voice came out hoarse. I pulled Lily with me toward the door. "I hear your mom."

That wasn't true, but I wanted Lily out of there.

Away from *her*.

"Lily, Kayla," I called. "Come on."

Surprisingly, they followed me into the hall. The air felt twenty degrees cooler out here.

Laura shut the door behind us, leaving her and the red-haired girl alone in the room.

"That was amazing," Lily gushed after Kayla left to find her parents and we returned to our room.

"What?" Lily's mom asked. "The view from the top? Did you see any animals?"

I could barely remember the hike. The red-haired girl crowded my brain.

Lily told her mom and aunt all about Laura and the ghost in room 22. As she'd predicted, Angela was all questions. "This will make a great angle for my article," she decided. "A haunted hotel. Perhaps it will make teens want to visit?"

I stayed quiet. No one noticed. With Lily, I was always the quieter one.

My thoughts shifted to Laura. Was she okay? Should I go back?

I chewed my lip. Mr. Himoff had hired Laura. This was her job, I reasoned. Not mine.

All during dinner—a cookout down by the lake—I watched for Laura. She never showed up.

After another night in the game room and a dance tournament that the girls rocked, Lily and I slid into our beds.

I lay back on the pillow and thought about that horrible heat that had covered my body.

"Sar? You awake?" Lily asked in the darkness.

"Yeah."

"I felt it today. The ghost. I felt it."

"What do you mean?"

"It's hard to explain." Lily kept her head on her pillow. "It was like a pull."

"A bad pull?" I remembered the anger. My fear that the girl would hurt Lily. That she wanted something from her.

"No." Her voice was heavy and already dreamy. "I think the ghost was looking for something. Do you believe me?"

"I do."

"I wish I knew more about the ghost. It's weird to feel something—to feel someone—and not know if it's a guy or girl, young or old."

I pressed my fingertips together. Should I describe the girl with the flame-colored hair and pitch-dark eyes? Should I explain the odd glow?

I could tell her everything.

"I think the ghost is a girl," I began.

"Me too."

"I kind of know it." I took a deep breath. "Remember how I came to live with Lady Azura last year? I never told you why. Well, I guess I sort of did. I told you that my dad needed help raising me. That's kind of true, but it's not the make-lunches-for-school, take-her-shopping kind of help. It's help that Lady Azura is good at because she has powers. Powers that let her see and talk to the dead. Powers that I have too. Powers that I was born with. I can"—I squeezed my eyes tight even though the room was dark—"see the dead and hear them and talk to them."

Lily said nothing.

My heart threatened to burst from my chest as I

waited. Was she so freaked out that she couldn't find anything to say?

"Lily?"

Nothing. The whir of the air conditioner filled the silence.

Tears pricked the corners of my eyes.

"Lil?"

I rolled over and, in the dim glow cast off from the bathroom, watched Lily's blanket move ever so slightly up and down. I heard her soft, rhythmic breathing.

Perfect. Just perfect.

I'd finally told her my secret, and she'd slept right through it.

Chapter 8

"Wyatt's gone," Kayla announced in a mysterious hush the next morning. We'd gathered under the canopied pavilion at the tennis courts for the teen clinic.

"Gone?" Lily cried.

"What happened?" I asked.

"Ghost attack." Owen made a slashing motion with his racquet.

"Seriously?" Lily sucked in her breath.

"Not seriously." Kayla snorted. "His dad had to go back to the city. Some office emergency. The whole family packed up and took off early this morning."

"Oh." Lily couldn't hide her disappointment.

Kayla wove her arm through Lily's. "Wyatt has the looks, but he's a pain. Trust me, no big loss. We'll hang. I'm so much more fun than silly Wyatt."

Lily grinned. "True."

"Clinic's starting." I pointed to the bald tennis pro waiting on the first court with one of those machines that fires balls at you. Four other kids waited with him.

Neither Lily nor Kayla seemed to hear me.

"I love your outfit!" Lily gushed. Kayla wore a graphic white-and-navy tennis dress with matching hat and socks.

Kayla pulled an identical hat from the huge tennis bag she carried. "I have two. You should wear it. We need to protect our skin from the sun."

Lily slipped it on. Kayla snapped a photo of their faces pushed together, grinning in their twin hats. I guess Kayla's concern about the sun didn't extend to my fair skin.

"Do you want to be partners?" Owen asked. "You know, if he pairs us up?"

Normally I'd be excited that a boy wanted to partner with me, but I was getting a strange vibe from Kayla. A vibe that made me want to be Lily's partner. I don't think I'm usually a very possessive person, but I was suddenly feeling really possessive over Lily. I didn't like the feeling.

"Sure," I said, unable to stop watching Kayla. She

was telling Lily a story about an audition. She had a way of touching Lily's shoulder every time she wanted to emphasize a point. She had a lot to emphasize. Every sentence seemed to have an exclamation point.

My phone buzzed. I hesitated, unsure if I should leave it on the bench and follow Owen out to the court. *It might be Dad,* I thought, reaching for it.

SO? A text from Mason.

SO NOTHING, I typed.

WHEN????

SOON.

"Who's that?" Kayla reached for my phone.

"No one." I grabbed my phone back.

"Ooh, do you have a secret?" she teased. "A secret boyfriend?"

"No." I clicked my phone off. "Just a friend."

"Who?" Lily asked. "Miranda?"

I didn't want to lie to her, and if I did, she'd find me out. Lily and I have the same friends. "Mason," I said.

"Really? Mason-who-used-to-own-my-dog Mason? I didn't know you guys texted."

"It's not a big deal."

"But he texts you? A lot?"

"Some," I admitted.

"Sara has a secret," Kayla crooned.

Lily considered this. "Does he like you?"

"No way," I said.

"I bet he does. Or you like him." Lily smiled. "I could totally see you guys together," she said loyally. "He's really cute," she told Kayla.

"That's not how it is," I insisted.

"Then how is it?" Lily asked. Not mean, just interested.

"Yeah, how is it then?" Kayla repeated what Lily said, only it did sound a little mean coming from her. Or was that just my imagination?

I hesitated, unsure what to say. This was the perfect opening for me to tell Lily. Except for the fact that Kayla was here.

"They're hiding their love," Kayla announced in a dramatic voice.

"No, you actually have no idea what you're talking about," I told Kayla, my voice betraying how tense I felt.

"New topic." Lily came to my rescue. She could tell I was getting upset. She told Kayla about feeling the pull of the spirit.

"We need to go back," Kayla insisted.

Lily shook her head. "There was a sign in the hallway this morning. Off-limits. Laura must've had Mr. Himoff post it after she caught us last night."

"Boring!" Kayla cried. "A sign is just words. Come on, no one will know." Lily chewed her lip. She wasn't much of a rule breaker.

"There's nothing to go back for," I pointed out.

"Don't be scared," Kayla said to me. Then she turned to Lily. "It's an adventure! We'll meet tonight at room twenty-two when the clock strikes midnight."

"I love little towns like this," Mrs. Randazzo commented as we strolled in and out of the stores lining the main street by the hotel.

"We live in a little town like this," Lily pointed out. "Stellamar has beachy tourist shops. This town has woodsy tourist shops. Shell paperweight. Moose paperweight. No difference."

"Big difference," her mom said. "I don't live here." She smiled broadly. "Check out how relaxed I am. Sara, back me up. Isn't everything different on vacation?"

Was it? I thought about Helliman House and the

spirit that waited for us in room 22. I'd come here to get away from haunted houses.

"It is, but—"

"Laura! Hey, Laura!" Lily called. She waved, and Laura glanced up from the store she was exiting. Dean's Natural Foods.

"Don't like the hotel food?" Angela asked as we met up with Laura.

"What? Oh, no. The food's quite tasty." Laura raised a recyclable canvas sack. "I needed supplies. Not to eat. For my job."

"What'd you get?" Lily poked her hand in the sack. Her mom gave her a look. "Sorry."

"No worries. It's not a secret." Laura pulled out each item. "Caraway seeds. Fennel. Sea salt."

"Dinner for the ghost?" Angela joked.

"A last supper, perhaps." Laura tilted her head, considering the idea. "With these ingredients, I'll create a charm to move the spirit on."

"You're going to run it out of the hotel?" Mrs. Randazzo asked, surprised.

"Not exactly. That's too harsh a way of looking at it. Spirits can't be forced out."

"So you somehow get them to move on?" Lily asked.

"Exactly! It's not out but on. With love and kindness, I encourage them to continue their journey." She raised her sack. "The caraway seeds and the fennel ward against evil. Sea-salt water combined with a pure heart makes the spirit more responsive to your wishes."

"I love your approach!" Lily clapped her hands.

"This is my first big job," Laura confided. After she said that, Angela looked at all of us and said, "So do you think I can trust her with our big secret?" After we all nodded, Angela told her about her article. Laura promised not to tell. She seemed happy not to be the only person working undercover at the hotel. "I'm a little nervous about all of this," she confided, but then added quickly, "I mean, I'm really good at sensing the presence of spirits. I help people break free from the expectations of dead relatives. So I'm sure I can do this, too."

"Have you ever gotten rid of a ghost?" I asked straight out.

"Not exactly," Laura admitted. "But I feel in my heart, I can. I'm heading there now."

I'd seen the ghost. Felt her negative energy. I doubted Laura's gentle approach would work. I reached in my pocket for my phone to call Lady Azura. She'd know what to do. She'd help me help Laura.

I touched the screen and hesitated. Lady Azura always cautioned me not to invite in trouble. She'd say this spirit hadn't bothered me, so why should I bother it?

She's right, I thought as I slipped my phone back into my pocket. Not my problem.

At midnight, I stood outside the door to room 22 with Lily and Kayla.

Kayla had texted countdowns to the not-to-be-missed event all evening. There'd been no way to stop Lily from sneaking out, so here I was watching her bounce on her toes with nervous excitement.

I'm not here to help Laura, I told myself. *I'm watching over Lily.*

Lily and I both wore pajama boxer shorts and tanks. Kayla had dressed in black leggings and a long-sleeved black shirt as if she were breaking into a bank. She touched Lily's shoulder in that familiar way. That possessive way.

Kayla reached for the knob. "It's open. Totally weird."

We scrambled inside and shut the door behind us. With the heavy drapes pulled closed, darkness blanketed the room. The sudden beam of a flashlight cut through the blackness. "Smart, right? We don't want anyone seeing a light under the door." Kayla seemed to have this sneaking-around thing all figured out.

The room looked the same in the thin shaft of light. Empty. Quiet. Cold.

Had Laura's herbal tricks worked? I wondered. I didn't feel anything. No tingling. Was the spirit gone?

And then . . .

Faint at first.

A glow in the corner.

A shimmer of orange light.

I strained my eyes against the shadows. Was the girl there? I couldn't see a body. Was she the glow?

"We should go back before your mother wakes up." I tried to sound calm, to pretend I hadn't seen anything. "Lily?"

Lily didn't answer. As if pulled by a magnet, she moved toward the corner with the glow. The glow grew brighter.

Lily stopped and stared blankly at the armchair slightly to the left of the glow.

"I'm bored. Hey, Lily, you sleepwalking?" Kayla moved alongside Lily and touched her shoulder.

The red-haired girl—suddenly as vivid as if she were still alive—shimmered into view.

"I think I feel something. Do you?" Lily's voice sounded strained.

"Yeah. Boredom," Kayla cracked. "This ghost is lame. Can't it at least moan or groan?"

"Don't be mean." Lily peered about. Her eyes never rested on the girl, her red hair eerily ablaze in the orange glow.

"I'm not," Kayla protested. "Let's do a midnight swim in the pool instead. We can easily climb that fence." She touched Lily's shoulder again.

The orange glow flared.

A rush of warmth burst under my skin.

The spirit flung her arm toward Kayla, knocking a brass reading lamp. It clattered into the armchair.

Kayla and Lily jumped back. For a moment, none of us spoke.

"Whoops!" Kayla said, breaking the silence and

righting the lamp. "I must've hit that."

We all knew she hadn't touched it.

At least, I knew.

The ghost girl glowed brighter. She glided closer to Lily.

"Time to go!" I reached for the doorknob and cried out in pain.

The knob was scalding hot!

Angry yellow flames licked the wooden door.

"What's up?" Lily asked, trying to move past me.

I couldn't let her. The door crackled with fire.

"Hey," she protested, then reached around me. Through the flames. And opened the door.

The fire was gone. Had it ever been there? Was I seeing things?

Tentatively, I touched the knob. Cool.

I glanced back. The girl was no longer visible.

"That room had nothing in it," Kayla complained.

Nothing, I thought, *but an angry orange glow in the corner.*

Chapter 9

I should have told her last night, I thought the next morning.

Lily twitched with nervous energy when we'd slipped unnoticed back into our room. "There's a ghost! I know it! I know it!" she kept repeating. "Why aren't you more excited?"

"I'm kind of used to it."

"Oh, right, Lady Azura," Lily said.

That's when I should've said something. But I was too tired to explain. Too tired to find the words to describe a spirit glowing orange.

I did the easy thing. I went to sleep.

I closed my eyes now as a woman with a neon-pink streak in her hair rubbed shampoo into my head. The suds had a pleasant citrus scent. I tried to enjoy the spa

treatments Angela had booked. *Relax,* I commanded myself as the woman massaged my head.

Not happening.

The secret was too big and getting bigger.

"Lily and Angela are down the hall with maple sugar scrub facials," Mrs. Randazzo said as I moved into the stylist chair next to hers. "I'm glad you chose to do the conditioning hair mask with me."

We sat together in our white-waffle spa robes and spa slippers as Zen-like music chirped from hidden speakers. Plastic wrap held a thick paste of milk and honey to our hair.

"Alone," Mrs. Randazzo murmured as the stylist left to bring us iced teas. "I love this hotel, but there are an awful lot of guests."

"Mmmm," I murmured.

The woman wore a robe just like ours. Foam dividers were wedged between her newly polished toes. She paced the room ducklike to keep her burgundy toenails from smudging. Her body shimmered, fading in and out.

I watched her move. I didn't have the tightening in my chest that I'd felt with the spirit in room 22. This woman was dead too, but she was happy and mellow.

"We're not alone here, are we?"

Mrs. Randazzo's voice was barely a whisper, yet I jumped. "Huh? What?"

"I saw that, Sara. I mean, I didn't see what I think you might have seen, but I watched your eyes. They saw someone, right?"

"I don't know what you're talking about," I protested, flustered. "It's just us."

"Sara." Lily's mom sounded as calm as she always did. "It's okay. You can talk to me."

"About what?"

"It must be a lot to hold inside." Her brown eyes filled with warmth. "Sara, I know," she added in a low voice.

"Know what?" I inspected my new turquoise manicure to avoid meeting her gaze.

"You're like your great-grandmother," she said simply. "You see spirits as well. I've known for a while, Sara. Your secret is safe with me. It always has been. It always will be."

"You don't care?" I blurted.

"Of course I care! But not in the way you mean. I

don't care that you have powers. That you're special."

"That I'm not normal."

"Actually, I find those of us not blessed with your heightened senses to be not normal. How can there be so much energy out there—the souls of so many people—that we can't see or feel?" She shook her head. "I envy you."

"You do?"

She swiveled my chair so I had no choice but to face her. "I've always believed that differences should be celebrated. Everyone brings something special to this world."

I had so many questions I wanted to ask. How did she know Lady Azura and I were alike? Who told her? But I didn't. Not because the stylist returned with our iced teas, but because I just wanted to enjoy this happy feeling.

She knew. She thought it was cool.

Two stylists washed out our masks, then brought us back to blow out our hair.

"Does Lily know?" I asked over the hum of the dryers.

"No. At least, not from me. I would never tell someone's secret."

My stylist twirled my chair, so I couldn't see the mirror while she curled and pinned up my hair. I faced a large window overlooking the lake.

"I want to tell Lily," I confided. I explained how I'd tried and failed. "Do I just blurt it out? Or do I lead into it slowly and kind of sneak it into a conversation?"

"Be like that sailboat out there." Lily's mom pointed to the white sail of a large boat gliding across the lake. "Read the wind."

"What wind?"

"The wind. Her emotions," she explained. "Sailors steer by the way the wind blows. Some days they go full-force ahead. Other days they zigzag slowly. To reach a port, though, you must sail, not drift."

Lily texted at that moment. She'd gone back to our room after her facial ended.

"Thank you," I told Mrs. Randazzo. I meant it more than I could even tell her right then. "I'm ready to sail!" I bolted out of the spa before I could change my mind and raced to our room.

"Lily!" I called, slipping my card key in and pushing open the door.

"Oh. My. God." Lily opened her mouth, closed it,

then burst out laughing. "Did you do that on purpose?"

"Do what?"

Lily led me to the mirror.

My eyes bulged as I viewed my hair for the first time. "I look like a toddler pageant queen crossed with a crazy wedding cake!" My blond hair, which usually hung long and straight, had been curled into a mess of tight corkscrews and then piled superhigh on my head.

"It's hysterical!" Lily cried. "America's Funniest Hairstyles."

"More like America's Worst Hairstyles!" I laughed. "A new reality show, starring me!"

"I so need to snap this."

"Use my phone." I struck silly poses as Lily took pictures with my cell.

"These are the best." Lily scrolled through the photos. "I've got to send them to Avery. Miranda, too."

"Go for it." I dug through my shellacked updo, trying to pull out the pins. "This requires octopus arms. Can you get the ones in the back?"

Lily peered intently at my phone. Her brows knit together. "Sara? What's all this?"

"All what?"

"You and Mason. You're texting about me. He keeps saying, 'Did you tell Lily?' and 'Does Lily know yet?'" She held the screen to my face. "Know *what*?" she demanded.

Deep breath.

"I've been trying to tell you for a long time. It's really hard to say."

"I'm listening."

With my hair still piled ridiculously on my head, I finally spilled the whole story. I told her about my powers, how I came to Stellamar so Lady Azura could help me understand them, and how I could see the dead.

"You mean, like, really see them? Face, body, expressions? The whole thing?" Lily asked.

"The whole thing. Hear them too."

"For real? Is this a joke? Are you filming me or something?"

It wasn't easy, but I convinced Lily that I wasn't pranking her. She had lots of questions. What it felt like (I got that tingling in my leg and sometimes felt sick), if it scared me (all the time), when I first saw one (when I was on the playground in preschool, but back then, everyone thought I had an imaginary friend), and why I didn't tell anyone (I didn't want to be one of those kids on the cover of the trashy magazines in the supermarket checkout lines).

"So?" I held my breath.

"So I think that's the most amazing, awesome thing ever!"

"For real?" I asked. "I've been so scared to tell you."

"Well, that was silly. I would never tell your secret. That's what best friends do, right? Just you and me on this one." She reached over and hugged me. "No more secrets ever, okay?"

And then I understood that weightless feeling that Mason talked about. I felt as if I'd been lifted high into the sky by a hundred helium balloons. My secret was no longer a rock in the pit of my stomach.

I hugged Lily back. "Just you and me," I agreed.

"Wait a second." Lily pulled away from me. "That's not right. Mason knew. Why did Mason know?"

"Well . . . uh . . . ," I fumbled.

"You barely know him. You told this huge secret to a boy you barely know before you told *me*?"

“It’s not like that.”

“You said telling me was this big thing. That no one else knew—”

“They don’t,” I protested.

“Mason does. You’ve seen him what, like, three times? I thought I was your best friend.”

“You are!” I’d promised Mason never to reveal his powers to move objects with his mind. But if I didn’t, how could I explain telling him before Lily? “It’s complicated. I can’t tell you why I told him. But it wasn’t really a choice. And that’s all I can say about it. I’m so sorry.”

“Another secret?”

“Yes,” I admitted.

“How many more do you have?”

“None. Really.”

Lily shook her head. “How can I be sure? You’re the only one who knows I sleep with a light on. When I had a crush on the lifeguard at the beach, I told only you. When my parents had that big fight last spring, I told only you. But you kept big secrets from me. You’re still keeping secrets.”

“There aren’t any more secrets. I promise!”

Lily studied me. "If I let the Mason thing go, that's it? Just you and me?"

"Maybe a ghost or two," I joked, trying to lighten the mood.

Lily smiled, despite trying not to.

"So no one else knows? Not even Jayden?"

Jayden had been my sort-of boyfriend last year at school, before his family moved away. I had wanted to tell him a million times but never had. I'd never really even come close to telling him. "Not even Jayden. I promise." Lily nodded, and I could tell we were going to be all right. I started telling her about my lessons with Lady Azura.

"Is your hair as silly as mine?" Lily's mom pushed open the door that connected our rooms. She eyed the two of us talking side by side on my bed. "Everything good here?"

I nodded eagerly.

Mrs. Randazzo's face lit up. She had the same contagious smile as Lily. "Excellent! Lily, I'm so glad Sara finally told you. It's mind-boggling, isn't it?"

"Wait. *You* know?" Lily stood between me and her mom. "About Sara?"

"Yes, sweetie, we've talked about it." Mrs. Randazzo sounded happy, almost relieved. She didn't notice the cloud descending over Lily's face. "I'll let you girls finish talking." She started to back out of the room and then caught my eye. "Everything is definitely good, right?"

"Right," I said, trying to force a smile.

"Yeah, we're good," Lily added in a voice that sounded so cheerful I almost believed her. "We just have to finish talking about some stuff." But the moment her mom left the room and shut the door, Lily turned to face me, and I knew she'd been acting for her mom's benefit. We most definitely were not good.

"You just told me that no one else knew." Lily's voice came out in a strangled whisper. She was hurt. I had hurt her.

"Why didn't you tell me you told *my mother* before me?" Lily demanded, her voice rising. "One more secret?"

"No, it wasn't a secret. I didn't think of it, that's all."

It sounded ridiculous, of course, but somehow, in the moment, I had totally forgotten about Mrs. Randazzo. I wished I had the power to somehow freeze time and go back and do it all over again. But that's one power I don't have.

"You forgot you told my mother before me, your supposed best friend? You promised, Sara." Her voice was heavy with hurt. "How many other people know? Really—just tell me the truth. Is everyone laughing at me? The dumb best friend? The only one who doesn't know you can see the dead?"

"No one else knows." This wasn't going the way I wanted. "You have to believe me."

"Believe what? That you can see ghosts? Or that you trust everyone but me to be cool with that info?"

"I trust you. I should've told you first." Tears pooled in my eyes. I'd been so afraid that Lily would laugh at me or not believe me or dump me as a friend. It had been all about how I would feel. I never thought I'd be the one to upset her.

"I'm so sorry," I said.

Lily crossed her arms. "Fine."

And I could tell from the look she gave me that we weren't fine. Not yet.

But I didn't know what else to say.

Chapter 10

Lily acted cold toward me for the rest of the day and into the night. After dinner, she didn't want to go to the teen dance party, so we rented a movie in our room. She watched it in silence.

I thought today would be better. I was wrong.

Breakfast was frosty. Lily spoke to me enough that her mom and Aunt Angela wouldn't be suspicious. But I knew she was still upset. And she knew I knew.

Give her time, I told myself. *Lily never stays angry for long.* Not that I knew this firsthand. Lily had never been angry with me. Until now.

She sat next to Kayla at the pool. I perched on a lounge chair in the "teen area" and watched as she had Kayla rub sunscreen on her back. That was my job. We always played a guessing game, painting letters or numbers on each other's backs.

Kayla described New York City stores I'd never heard of, and she promised to take Lily shopping when she came to visit. She, not we. Kayla didn't seem to care about why Lily was being cold to me. She was happy to have the spotlight of Lily's full attention.

Give her time, I told myself again.

"I'm taking a walk," I announced. "Want to come?"

"No, thanks. We're going to chill here." Kayla settled back on her chair. Lily flipped down her sunglasses and leaned back too, letting Kayla decide for her.

Okay, then. I knew when I wasn't wanted.

I wandered the grounds of Helliman House. Groomed paths wove through groves of pine trees. Little signs described different ferns, birds, and flowers along the way. I tried to read them, but my mind was still with Lily.

The path led me around the side of the hotel. Spotting a door propped open by a large painted stone, I entered. A short hall with several offices opened into the main lobby. I stopped suddenly when I heard a familiar childlike voice.

"I need more information," Laura pleaded from the

other side of the door marked PRIVATE.

"What more can I give?" a man replied.

"I can't help until I know who I am dealing with and why he or she is here," Laura explained.

"That's your job." The man sounded gruff.

"I know." Laura let out an exasperated sigh. "I cleansed the area, but I still feel a presence. Do you know if we're dealing with many ghosts or just one?"

"No idea. Listen, Laura, can you do this or do I need to get someone else?" He didn't hide his annoyance. "A huge wedding party arrives tomorrow. We're fully booked. I need those rooms. I can't lose this business. You have twenty-four hours to get those ghosts gone, and not a minute more. And I'm not paying you a cent until you do."

The door swung open, and I stepped away. Laura walked out. For a moment, I thought about slipping unnoticed into the bustle of the lobby. Then I saw her rub her temples. "Are you okay?" I asked.

She was surprised to see me. "Not so much," she admitted. She told me everything I'd overheard. "It's not about the money. It's about my reputation as a spiritual healer. I want to do the job I was hired to do, but I need to understand the spirit better so I can find the right herb to banish it."

"Understand how?" I asked as we strolled through the lobby.

"Who it is. Why it's still here." Laura stopped before one of the walls of old photos. "Spirits stay behind for a reason."

Should I tell her? I wondered. I could describe the red-haired girl. I could tell her about the glow. About the flames. But if I did, I'd have to reveal my powers. Tell another person. I felt, somehow, the right thing to do would be to run the idea by Lily before blurting it out to Laura.

I examined the photos with Laura. The lake with a small boat with an old-fashioned outboard motor. The original house with a boxy, black car in the circular drive. Suitcases were strapped to the back of the car. No trunks in those days, I figured.

Then I sucked in my breath.

The girl with the red hair. Except it wasn't red now. In the photo, there were only shades of black, white, and gray. But I didn't need to see the crimson hair to know it was her.

She posed in a dark dress in a stiff family portrait. The photo had been taken in front of the stone fireplace that now graced the lobby. She stood with her mother and father and a younger, dark-haired girl, who looked about thirteen. I thought she might be the girl I'd seen in my vision. The girl on the bed with her older sister.

"Who are they?" I asked.

Laura didn't know. She motioned over Sofia, who'd been straightening flower arrangements on the side tables.

"That's the Helliman family," Sofia reported. "The original owners of the house. Andrew Helliman and his wife, May. The older daughter was named Belinda, and the younger one was Margaret."

"What happened to them?" I asked.

"They all died in a fire that destroyed part of the house."

"That's so horrible." Laura shuddered. "Those poor souls." The fire I'd seen and felt now made sense.

Laura brushed her fingertips along the portrait. "Those poor souls," she repeated. Then she turned to me. "I think we found the ghosts who are haunting the hotel. It's a whole family!" She hurried toward the open elevator. "I need to prepare for a cleansing," she called over her shoulder before the door shut, whisking her away.

Laura's close, I thought with relief. I wanted her to figure it out. It wasn't the whole family in room 22. It was just Belinda. I stared at the portrait. She gazed dreamily into the distance.

Why? I thought. *Why are you still here, Belinda?*

Only an inch separates giving someone their space and shutting them out, I decided. Enough time had passed. I headed back to the pool.

I had a plan. A really simple one. I'd tell Lily that I was sorry a million times until I got her to forgive me. Even if Kayla refused to budge from Lily's side, I'd keep apologizing.

I spotted Lily and her mom standing around a tall table by the frozen yogurt stand. Kayla was nowhere in sight. Lily held her yogurt, not eating it. Her mother talked, waving her arms as she spoke. I'd been at their house enough to know the waving arms meant she was upset.

Now wasn't the time for my one million sorrys. I detoured down a path that led to the lake to give them their privacy. Instead of turning right to the dock and the roped-off swimming area, I headed left. The path followed the curve of the lake. Through the reeds along the shore, I watched a family of ducks paddle nearby.

The land jutted into a lake, forming a small peninsula. At the tip, under a lone pine, a wooden bench with chipped gray paint faced the water. I touched the metal plaque affixed to the back. SITE OF ORIGINAL BOATHOUSE. DESTROYED BY FIRE IN 1922.

No boathouse stood here now.

I was alone, except for the ducks.

Sitting on the bench, I stared out at the dark-blue lake. The water was so calm compared with the churning Atlantic waves of home. I missed home. I missed talking with Lady Azura. She'd know what to do about the red-haired girl. She'd know what to do about Lily. I was messing everything up—or at least, not doing anything to fix it.

The midday sun beat down on my face, and the rhythmic lap of the lake against the rocky edge made me suddenly sleepy. I gazed over the water, unable to focus. The surrounding pines grew fuzzy. Their crisp needles blurred into a watercolor. The blue of the water blended with the blue of the sky. A swirl of blues and greens.

At the end of the point, I saw a boathouse. A boathouse that I was positive wasn't there before.

White wood with a pointed roof. The shape of a house a young child draws.

I blinked rapidly to clear my vision.

The boathouse remained.

A shiver worked its way down my back.

Standing, I wandered toward the boathouse. Was it real?

A rowboat bobbed in the water at the end of a long, narrow dock. A rope knotted to a post kept it from floating away. Two girls sat in the boat. They didn't see me, even though I stood out in the open. Who were they? Where had they come from?

The girls wore long dresses cinched at the waist with long, puffy sleeves. One had a wide-brimmed hat with fake flowers, and the other held a thin ruffled umbrella. A parasol, I thought. The parasol-girl's long, dark hair gleamed in the sunlight. She reached out with her free hand and grasped the other girl's hand, said something, and then laughed. An infectious giggle that glided toward me.

A sound I'd heard before.

The girl tilted her parasol and turned, still not seeing me.

Margaret Helliman.

The younger sister.

The younger dead sister.

If she was here and so was I, what did this mean? I struggled to breathe as I gaped at her.

Laughter fell from her face as her eyes went wide with disbelief. I followed the path of her gaze to the boathouse. To Belinda. Her sister.

Belinda stood stiffly with her arms crossed and feet planted wide apart. Her red hair flew across her face in the breeze. Her eyes scared me. They blazed with jealousy.

The more I stared at her, the more I could feel it. The hurt that Margaret was laughing with someone else. That Margaret had chosen someone else. That they were laughing at me.

Belinda's eyes turned as red as her hair.

A dark, angry red.

And then I smelled it. Burning wood. The bitter, sweet scent of a campfire.

Belinda didn't move. The aroma of smoke grew stronger. Then wood cracked, and I saw the glow of flames. Real flames. Flames licking at the corners of the small boathouse. Flames growing larger and larger.

Belinda raised her hands to her mouth in horror. Her eyes were no longer red. Tears streamed down her cheeks, and her shoulders shook.

Quickly dropping her dainty parasol, Margaret unknotted the rope, releasing the boat from the dock, and grabbed the oars. Then she rowed away to safety.

Away from her sister.

Belinda wailed alone as the boathouse burned.

Chapter 11

A ringing echoed in my ears. Sirens? Fire trucks on their way? The boathouse was long past saving, and Belinda had run past me and up the grassy hill leading to the large house.

The ringing again.

From my pocket.

I looked down, confused.

I sat on a bench.

The air smelled of pine and lake water.

The fire was gone.

It hadn't been real. Or it had, but it'd happened long ago. A vision into the past. Belinda's past.

My phone kept ringing, so I pulled it out and answered it.

"Hello, Sara."

"Lady Azura!" I cried with relief.

"I sensed turmoil. Troubles. The need for a friendly voice," she said in her raspy voice. A voice I'd missed.

"You're right." I sighed, then told her all about Belinda, Margaret, and Laura. I didn't let on that Lily wasn't talking to me. That hurt too much to say out loud.

"I have encountered spirits with great heat around them a few times before." I heard her fingernails tap the side of her armchair as she thought. "They are very dangerous. Very unpredictable."

"But heat and that glow around her, that was different from the vision I just had," I said. "She was standing there, and the boathouse burst into flames."

"It's possible Belinda can start fires with her mind."

"Do you mean she just thinks about it and *poof*?"

"I don't think she plans to start a fire. She's guided by her emotions. If you are angry, you may scream. For her, anger and fear bring on fire. It's called pyrokinesis."

"She was jealous. Very jealous." I didn't have to explain to Lady Azura that sometimes a spirit's feelings felt like they were mine.

"Pyrokinesis is extremely difficult to control, especially for someone so young," she said. "Especially if no adult understands what is happening. I doubt one hundred years ago poor Belinda had much support."

For the longest time, every time a spirit appeared I'd been petrified. No one knew about what I could do. "I don't think she knows how to control her power." I thought back to the orange glow and her blazing eyes. "That makes her dangerous."

"I need you to promise you will stay far away from this spirit," Lady Azura instructed.

I promised.

"You and Lily both," she added.

I couldn't promise for Lily. I finally told her what had happened between us.

"She's upset. That's understandable." Lady Azura paused, not going down the I-told-you-so path. "What does Lily's friendship mean to you?"

"Everything." I didn't hesitate. I'd never had a friend like her before.

"Then forget the spirit. Fight for her friendship."

I returned to the pool. Lily lay on the chaise lounge by herself. Kayla stood in a long line for frozen yogurt.

"Hey," I said, gathering strength from Lady Azura's advice.

"Hey." Lily didn't look up from her magazine.

I glanced at the cover. Lily and I had read that one together yesterday while getting pedicures at the spa. She was only using it to hide.

"Listen," I said. "I'm so, so sorry. Seriously."

Lily peeked over the top of the magazine.

"Incredibly sorry." I unclasped my necklace and slid off the aragonite bead. "This is for you. For your necklace." I'd given Lily her own necklace with a crystal for her birthday.

I placed the reddish-brown crystal in her palm.

"What's it for?" she asked.

"Friendship."

She rolled the bead with her fingertip, then threaded it onto her necklace.

I smiled. It was enough. A beginning.

"Can you believe they ran out of the chocolate crunchy things?" Kayla pouted and thrust her yogurt cup toward us. "Now all my toppings will have that same soft feeling in my mouth. Totally changes the experience."

"You could try granola," I suggested. I'd decided to be extra nice to Kayla. If Lily liked her, I'd try too.

"Granola tastes like oats they feed to a horse." Kayla reclined on the cushioned chaise next to Lily.

I shrugged and perched on the end of Lily's chair. Lily pulled up her feet to make room. A good sign.

"Laura was just here," Lily said.

"Really? How's she doing with everything?" It felt weird to tiptoe into a conversation with Lily.

"Good." Lily fidgeted with the frames of her sunglasses.

"She invited us to one of her cleansings tonight." Kayla filled in what Lily had been hesitant to say. "Room twenty-two again. She told us about the Helliman family dying in that fire. She wants to use us as bait."

"Not as bait," Lily turned to Kayla. "That sounds so crude."

"Bait?" I repeated.

"Yes, *bait*." Kayla emphasized the word. "She wants to catch the ghosts, and she says she only feels them when we're there. So she wants us to hang out in the room, like *bait*, to lure the big, bad ghosts."

"It's not a joke, Kayla," Lily said quietly. "I felt something in that room. Laura agrees."

"Don't do it," I said.

"Why not?" Kayla demanded.

I studied Kayla for a moment. Had Lily told her about

my powers? No, I decided. Lily had kept my secret.

"It *feels* wrong." I trained my gaze on Lily. I hoped she'd understand.

"Laura needs me. She told me so," Lily said quietly. I could tell she had her mind made up, but so did I.

"It's a mistake," I repeated stubbornly.

"Are you scared?" Kayla asked. "'Cause I'm not scared to chill in the haunted room."

"We're going tonight," Lily told me. "You can take a pass, if you want."

"It's not about me." It was about Lily and the red-haired ghost. I didn't know why, but when Lily was around, the spirit got that dangerous orange glow. "Lily, I need to talk to you about this."

"So talk," Kayla chimed in.

"It's private," I said pointedly.

Lily sighed. "Sara, I get that you're trying to help, but you're not going to change my mind. I felt that spirit in that room. I know I did. Laura needs *me*, and I promised her."

"You can't!" I was desperate to keep Lily away. "I won't let you. I'll . . . I'll tell your mom you're planning to sneak out again!"

Both Lily's and Kayla's eyes widened. Instantly, I knew that I'd said the stupidest thing.

"What's with you and my mom?" Lily demanded, unable to disguise her hurt. "You two like talking behind my back, is that it?"

"No, that's not it. I didn't mean—"

"I don't care what my mom thinks." Lily stood abruptly. "Friends support each other. They don't tattle."

"But I would never. I just said that because—"

"Kayla, I'm really warm. Let's swim." Lily stalked toward the waterslide with Kayla close on her heels.

I buried my head in my hands. I only wanted to help my best friend. Why was it all going so wrong?

I looked up at Kayla and Lily whispering in line by the stairs to the slide. I should be by Lily's side, not Kayla. Lily barely knew this girl.

Then I heard Lily's infectious giggle.

A sound so familiar.

A sound that now made my blood run cold.

I'd heard that sound in my visions. By the boathouse and in the bedroom. The giggle of Margaret Helliman.

Lily and the dead girl had the same giggle.

What did that mean?

Chapter 12

I hugged my knees in the darkness and sucked in my breath. Footsteps echoed eerily down the empty hall, growing louder and louder. My heart pounded as she approached.

"No! No!" I wanted to scream. I peeked through my fingers. My hands were ready to cover my eyes.

"Don't do it," Owen murmured under his breath. "Don't open that door."

She didn't listen.

Her pale hand twisted the doorknob. Owen's body stiffened next to me. The door creaked on its hinges.

For a moment, there was silence.

And then screams. Shrill, terrified screams. From her. From me. From voices all around me. Tentacles lashed out. A big, bulbous head with one eyeball and teeth. Lots of jagged teeth.

I ripped the paper 3-D glasses off my face. “A sea monster that walks on land? Really?”

“Totally. Oh! Watch out!” Owen called to the girl on the oversize movie screen set up by the lake. Nearly strangled, the girl ripped the attacking tentacle, and green slime squirted out.

“Gross,” Owen murmured.

We shared one of the many plaid blankets scattered across the grass for Teen Scary Movie Night. *Creature from the Deep* was playing. I wondered about the wisdom of this choice. How many of the kids surrounding me in the chilly night would brave the dark lake water tomorrow, even with the sun shining bright?

Not me.

I glanced to my right to see Lily’s reaction. She was easily freaked out by scary movies.

She wasn’t there.

By the pale moonlight, the blanket that she’d shared with Kayla lay empty.

“Where are they?” I nudged Owen, who still gaped at the struggle on the screen.

“Sneaked off. Before the scene with the mist.”

How’d I miss that?

The girl on the screen screamed again. "Run!" Owen cried, shaking his mop of curls in disbelief. I didn't bother to follow the horror she'd let herself in for now. My eyes searched the sloping lawn for Lily and Kayla.

I knew I wouldn't find them outside.

I knew where they'd gone.

Without me.

I debated staying on the blanket and watching the end of the movie. But I didn't care if the sea monster ate the girl or not.

I did care about Lily.

"Be right back," I whispered to Owen. Then I made my way up to the hotel.

To the second floor.

To room 22.

The door was ajar. Laura, Lily, and Kayla stood between the two beds. I leaned against the door frame and watched Laura. She dipped her fingertips into a shallow bowl, then scattered liquid onto the carpet. Lily remained motionless, and Kayla rocked on her heels as they watched Laura chant, *"Fire, fire burning bright. Leave us, leave us tonight."*

Belinda watched too, from the far corner. The salt water or whatever Laura sprinkled had no effect on her.

Laura looked up and motioned me inside.

"I thought you didn't—" Kayla began, but Laura shushed her.

Lily said nothing.

The air felt thick and stuffy, even though the door wasn't closed. I joined them in the center. The temperature grew warmer.

"Can you feel the heat?" Laura whispered.

"No." Kayla inspected her cuticles.

Lily nodded and so did I.

"Are there . . . are there ghosts here?" Lily asked.

Was she talking to me?

"Yes," Laura answered. "There is one. I feel the presence of one."

I hadn't realized I'd been holding my breath until I exhaled deeply. Laura knew! She was going to be okay. She could handle this.

"What happens next?" I whispered.

Laura placed the bowl on the night table. "Next, we form the circle of banishment."

"What's that?" Kayla asked.

"Hold hands. All of us," Laura instructed.

I kept my eyes on the shimmery form of Belinda as I grasped Laura's and Kayla's hands. Sweat beaded along my hairline.

"I brought a special oil lamp with an extra-long wick. We will set it on a table in the middle of our circle to burn," Laura continued.

"Burn?" I squeaked.

"Shhh," Lily warned me.

"Laura, remember what Sofia said? Don't you think anything with fire is a bad idea?" I didn't know much about what was going on, but I knew striking a match near Belinda was asking for trouble.

Laura considered this for a moment. "Agreed. No oil lamp."

"What'd you do when you cleansed other houses?" I asked.

"This is my first. We'll go with the circle approach." Laura pursed her lips.

I cringed. *Her first time.* Laura was making this up as she went along.

Lily watched me react from directly across our circle. I couldn't tell what she was thinking.

"Let's sit," Laura instructed. "Keep a strong grip and close your eyes. Focus on banishing the spirit within these walls." She began to hum.

Kayla and Lily closed their eyes along with her. There was no way I was going to stop watching Belinda. Already the faintest orange glow had appeared around her.

Their humming was slightly off-key and increased in volume. Belinda glided toward our circle.

Toward Lily.

Sweat snaked down my neck, pooling in the hollow of my collarbone. Belinda hovered behind Lily. Gently, her hand stroked Lily's hair. Up and down, as if brushing her long waves.

The room grew warmer.

Lily's eyelids fluttered open. She zeroed in on my horrified expression. *Ghost?* she mouthed.

I nodded, afraid to anger Belinda with a sudden movement.

Lily stayed eerily calm. *Where?* she mouthed.

Behind you, I mouthed back, my body rigid with fear. My skin prickled with heat. Hotter and hotter. *Don't move.*

Belinda leaned closer, twisting a strand of Lily's hair around her finger. Lily remained frozen.

Kayla dropped my hand. "Okay, it's like a thousand degrees in here, and nothing's happening. This is stupid." She stood and stepped away. Then she pulled her phone from the pocket of her faded zip-up sweatshirt and scrolled through texts.

Laura opened her eyes and frowned.

Belinda dropped Lily's hair but stayed where she was.

"Lil, they're serving ice cream down by the lake. Mint chip." Kayla was clearly bored. "Let's get out of here." She reached down to pull Lily upright.

Belinda's eyes blazed. The glow around her deepened. She pushed on Lily's shoulder, holding her down as Kayla tried to pull her up. Lily let out a muffled cry.

"What's wrong? You coming?" Kayla asked.

"Not now," Lily managed. She shot me a desperate look. Belinda held her in place.

I couldn't tear my eyes away from Belinda's hand on Lily. My skin seared with the pain of blistering sunburn.

"That cute boy texted me. The one from the

waterslide." Kayla held out her phone.

Lily glanced between me and Kayla. "Later," she said tightly.

"I'm going to get ice cream with him. Meet us, okay?" Kayla headed out into the hall, all the while typing on her phone.

My throat was so dry I could barely push out the words. "Go," I croaked. "Go with Kayla."

Lily shook her head.

"She's touching you," I said. "She wants you to be with her. You have to get out now."

"I know," Lily whispered. "I can sort of feel her. I wish I could see her like you."

"See her?" Laura's head twisted from Lily to me. "What do you mean? Sara, you can *see* her?"

Chapter 13

I told Laura what I could do. There wasn't time for an in-depth sharing, since Belinda still hovered beside Lily, but Laura got the idea.

Mostly.

"We need to combine our energies." She gripped my hand tightly. "Is she by Lily?"

"Yes." Only one-word answers for me. I had to watch Belinda.

"Be gone, be gone, it is your time to move on," Laura chanted. She jutted her chin at me to join in.

"Be gone." I repeated it several times, each one more forceful than the one before. Belinda's eyes blazed as my voice grew louder. I didn't care. I wanted her away from Lily. The aura around her radiated. My skin seared, but I refused to back down. "Be gone!"

Eyes red, Belinda wrapped her shimmery arms

around Lily. She pulled Lily toward her, squeezing tighter and tighter. Lily's face drained of color. She began to wheeze, fighting for air.

Belinda tightened her grip.

"Stop it, Belinda! Get away!" I screamed. What was I thinking? I couldn't control this spirit. She was much more powerful than I was. I scrambled frantically toward Lily.

"Belinda?" Lily's voice was so normal-sounding that I stopped. "Belinda, can you hear me?"

"What are you—?" I began, but Lily spoke over me.

"Belinda, is this your bedroom? It's so pretty. I love how you can see the sun set over the lake." Lily twisted around and forced a smile.

Belinda loosened her hold, clearly captivated by the melody of Lily's words.

"You are so pretty. Does everyone tell you that?" Lily continued.

The crimson dimmed from Belinda's eyes as she listened to Lily.

"Go on," I whispered. Laura nodded, clearly confused by the turn of events.

"You must have so much fun here by the lake," Lily said.

"Maggie . . . oh, Maggie!" a strained cry escaped from Belinda's pale lips.

I looked to Laura and Lily. Neither heard her.

Belinda trembled as she repeated the name. Then she touched Lily's hair again and cried, "Play with me, Maggie."

"What's going on?" Laura hissed, reaching for my shoulder.

"Belinda thinks Lily's her sister," I whispered.

"Margaret?" Laura asked.

"She calls her Maggie." I hesitated, not wanted to freak Lily. "She's touching your hair. She wants to *play* with you."

"Oh, I'd love to play, Belinda. Just you and me." Lily didn't miss a beat. She didn't sound scared, although I couldn't figure out why. "But I am not Maggie. My name is Lily Randazzo. Maggie is your sister, right?"

The temperature of the room dropped at the mention of her sister.

"I'm not Maggie." Lily leaned forward. "Maggie died a long time ago."

The once-dark TV screen suddenly crackled to life, filling the room with a white static buzz. The digital clock on the bedside table blinked rapidly. *10:14. 10:14. 10:14.* Through the bathroom door, we heard the shower turn on with a rush of water.

Belinda pulled her arms into herself and raised her shoulders. Her red hair fanned out as the glow returned, more intense than before.

"She's upset," I said. My skin once again burned with her emotions.

"We need to leave," Laura announced hastily above the roar of the TV and the shower.

"No, not yet," Lily protested.

"I can't do it." Laura's voice trembled as she watched the clock flash the same number over and over. "I can't fix this problem."

"Laura's right," I agreed. "She's going to hurt us." I should've listened to Lady Azura, I realized. We never should have messed with this spirit.

"It's locked!" Laura cried as she tried desperately to twist the doorknob. "It shouldn't be locked, but it is!"

"Sara, look!" Lily pointed toward the floor. Thin wisps of smoke snaked up from beneath the door.

I raced to the window and tried to pry it open. It wouldn't budge. I struggled with the wooden frame as the heat deepened around us.

"Don't waste time. We need to break it," Laura commanded from behind me. She pulled off her leather clog and began to pound at the pane with the rubber-soled heel.

"I can't breathe," I rasped. Tears welled in my eyes.

"Wet a washcloth! Put it over your face!" Laura cried.

I wanted to run to the bathroom, but I couldn't move. All I could do was stare at Belinda as my stomach churned. Her body shone, as if the glow were illuminated from within her. Her fists balled at her sides, and she stared with a burning intensity.

I felt her anger. Her disappointment. Her grief. So many emotions boiling at the surface.

So much pain.

I remembered what Lady Azura said. Her emotions caused her to start fires.

"She's upset about her sister." I coughed. Smoke stuck in my throat. "We need to calm her!"

Laura continued to smack the glass harder, but Lily

turned toward where I pointed. "It's okay, Belinda. I'm here. You're not alone. We can be friends. . . ."

Lily's voice grew fuzzy as thick smoke filled my eyes. I tried to see the spirit's reaction to Lily's words, but everything turned hazy and began to spin. My knees buckled and my body swayed. Then the smoke covered me like a blanket, and I closed my eyes.

Chapter 14

Dust tingled my nose, causing me to sneeze. I squinted into the glare of the late afternoon sun. Reds, oranges, and yellows filled the cloudy sky. The colors of fire.

But there was no fire. No more smoke.

Trees surrounded me with their autumn leaves ablaze. I stared in wonder at the fat maple leaves dripping from the branches. A rhythmic *clip-clop* on the other side of an iron fence revealed a tan horse pulling a wagon and kicking up dust on a city street.

The laughter of young children reached my ears. I stood in a school yard with girls wearing long dresses, big bows in their hair, and lace-up boots. Boys dressed in tweed pants and jackets.

Where was I?

"Lily?" I twisted, searching.

A small girl ran from the crowd. Her red hair blew

behind her as she dodged their jeers. A stone sailed toward her. Then another. The children threw rocks and taunted her.

The girl barreled toward me. Her tiny hands balled into fists. Her face scrunched in hurt and fear. Tears streamed down her cheeks.

I opened my arms to her.

And then I stood in a sweet-smelling bedroom with yellow wallpaper and tall windows. On a four-poster bed, a regal woman with dark hair twisted in a bun gathered the red-haired child from the playground in her arms.

"Mama, no one will be my friend. No one!" the girl wailed.

The mother smoothed her daughter's tangles. "It's only because they are afraid of what you do." The mother tried to mask her own sadness. "Do not fret. You have your sister. She will always be your friend."

And then I stood outside on a sloping lawn bordered by majestic pines. Beside me two girls played with porcelain-faced dolls. The red-haired girl was older now, maybe ten. The slight, dark-haired girl beside her looked younger. A whistle caught their attention. A boy in overalls kicked a stone down the nearby road. He spotted the girls. "Freak!" he called. "Freak!"

"Don't listen, Belinda," the younger girl soothed.

The red-haired girl's face had already crumbled. Color rose to her cheeks as the boy continued to cry, "Freak!"

In a shower of sparks that made me jump, her doll burst into a bonfire. Fire ate at the doll's petticoats and satin dress, then slowly moved to singe the moss-green grass.

Belinda now sat on a moss-green sofa with her hands folded on her lap. Older still, maybe sixteen, her hair held back in a braid.

Across from her sat the regal woman and a heavyset man with a turned-up mustache. Andrew and May Helliman. His face was grave. Hers was tearstained.

"It's the only way." Belinda's mother twisted a lace handkerchief as she spoke. "Cousin Katherine has agreed to take you. I hear her cottage in Bristol, England, is quite nice."

"I don't want to be sent away! I don't want to go to

England. I don't know this cousin." Belinda couldn't control her tears.

"It's not a choice." Her father refused to look directly at his daughter. "The doctor said it's the only way. After that boathouse fire . . . everyone knows you're a danger, Belinda."

"You and Margaret are all I have!" Belinda wailed. "I promise not to start more fires. I promise!"

"The doctor said the only other choice is to have you locked up." Mrs. Helliman pressed her handkerchief to her eyes. "We can't do that. You *must* leave."

"I won't!" Belinda said defiantly. Her expression had hardened. "You can't make me!"

Her father rose to his full height, towering over his teenage daughter. "Yes, I can." He gripped her arm and dragged her out of the room and upstairs. "You go first thing in the morning."

The lock on her bedroom door clicked loudly from the outside. Belinda tried twisting the knob desperately, but the door wouldn't budge.

There was no way out until morning. Until she was sent away.

Suitcases, already packed by one of the Helliman

servants, lay waiting by the door of her bedroom with the pink-flowered wallpaper. Belinda crawled to the wall and knocked four times. Her secret signal to her sister.

Margaret returned the knocks from her bedroom on the other side. Belinda pleaded through the thin wall for Margaret to unlock her door. They'd run away together.

Margaret kept repeating, "I'm sorry." She couldn't or wouldn't open the door. She told Belinda to sleep.

"No!" Belinda howled. As she moaned, her hair took on a darker hue. Redder. Angrier.

No longer in control.

They couldn't send her away. By herself.

Red everywhere.

No Margaret. No friends.

All she saw was a curtain of red.

Until the suitcases burst into flames.

Belinda watched in awe as the yellow fingers of heat grew higher and higher. It was as if she were in the audience, viewing a play on a far-off stage. Then the flames leaped to the windowsill, igniting the wood with a ferocity that shocked her into action.

"Wake up! Everyone get out!" She grabbed a cotton blanket folded at the foot of her bed and flung it in hopes of putting out the fire. The blanket disappeared into the flames.

Into the flames that engulfed the bedroom.

Into the flames that traveled down the hall to the bedrooms where her family slept.

"It's all her fault," I said. I'd seen Belinda start the fire that killed her family.

"No, it's not."

I blinked. I was back in the hotel room. Smoke everywhere. Laura still struggling with the window.

Lily pressed a cool washcloth to my face as I sat on the carpet. The TV static, the shower, and the blinking clock had stopped. How long had I been like this?

"It's not her fault," Lily repeated. "I don't know where you went in your mind, Sara, but you were talking the whole time. Narrating what you saw."

I pulled the washcloth away and eyed Belinda, still hovering beside Lily. "It was bad. She did it."

"No. It was a mistake," Lily said simply. "Belinda didn't mean to start that fire or any of the fires. She had no control. She needed help that no one could give her."

"That's what's so dangerous." I couldn't shake the image of those flames.

"She's lonely, Sara. She lost her family and her sister. She needs a friend—that doesn't make her bad. Everyone judged her unfairly."

The smoke drifted away. Belinda's clenched jaw softened. Laura stepped from the window and moved toward the door.

I thought about all the times I'd been quick to judge. I'd thought Delilah was destructive when she'd really been baking muffins. I'd thought George Marasco wanted to destroy Midnight Manor on the boardwalk when he'd really wanted to save it. I thought the soldier spirit was trying to spook me when he'd really wanted to find Lady Azura, his true love. Had I been wrong about Belinda?

"She may be lonely, but she starts fires," I said. "She scares me."

"Even though you can see her and I can't," Lily said, "I know what I feel when she's near, and I don't feel scared. I want to help her."

"Take me home," Belinda said in a low voice. Her glow had dimmed. She searched Lily's face with her now-dark eyes. "Take me home with you."

"She wants to go home with *you*," I told Lily.

"It's open!" Laura cried with a giddy laugh. The door suddenly swung open, ushering in a rush of cool air. "Let's get out."

"I'm not leaving without her," Lily said.

Laura waved us to hurry. "Who? Sara?"

"Belinda."

"Whoa!" Laura lifted her arms in protest.

"Sara?" Lily asked. She raised her eyebrows, and I knew what she wanted.

"I don't know if I can," I admitted.

"Please." Lily said. "I trust you."

I nodded. I'd try.

I never, ever thought we'd be doing *this* together. But what else can you do when your best friend needs help?

Chapter 15

Except for the faint smell of ash, the room had magically cleared of smoke. Belinda remained by Lily's side. Laura stayed by the door. I watched Belinda warily. Without the glow and the burning eyes, she looked like any other teenager in an old-fashioned nightgown. With a change of clothes, I could imagine her hanging out at the boardwalk arcade back home.

That's how I'd talk to her, I decided. None of Laura's new age chants. None of Kayla's snippy remarks. None of the fear and taunts of those other kids.

"Lily likes you," I began. "We both do."

Lily nodded her encouragement. "Tell her that we can be friends, but she can't come live with me."

I did. "You need to find your family," I added. "Your parents and your sister. They're waiting for you to join them."

"They do not want me," Belinda replied.

"That's silly," Lily scoffed when I translated. "Your parents were listening to some silly doctor. Your mother was so sad and overwhelmed that day. She thought sending to you to your cousin would help. Margaret only wanted what was best for you too."

"They wanted me to be alone." Belinda's voice had a flat, hollow sound.

I needed to try something else. How could I ask this girl to leave this room and this world without giving her something to go to? Watching Lily stare in the opposite direction from where Belinda stood, I realized she needed *someone*.

I closed my eyes and focused on Margaret. I brought forward all the visions I'd seen of her and tried to connect. Tried to will her back to this world.

A hand tapped my shoulder.

Lily pointed to the aragonite crystal on her necklace. "Can I?" she asked.

"Definitely."

Lily slid off the bead, and I pointed to the corner where Belinda hovered. Moving slowly, Lily gently placed the crystal on the ground. "This means friendship. Sara gave it to me, and I'm giving it to you."

Belinda bent down and scooped up the crystal, making a protective cup with her hands. She stared incredulously at it.

"She took it," I whispered.

Lily let out a nervous giggle of relief.

The sound of her laugh. Same as Margaret's laugh. I focused on their similar happiness.

I let the sound fill me. Surround me.

My left foot began to tingle. That pins-and-needles feeling I dreaded—until now. I looked about with anticipation. And then Margaret materialized, her nightgown-clad body barely visible.

For a moment, the two sisters stared at each other.

I waited, unsure of what to say or do. Laura moved alongside me and placed her hand on my shoulder, as if she knew.

Slowly, Margaret opened her arms to invite her sister in. Belinda melted into her hug.

And then they were gone.

I stared at the empty corner. No sisters. No glow. Only the aragonite crystal remained, nestled in the carpet.

"You did it!" I wrapped Lily in a similar hug. "She's gone!"

"Is she happy?" Lily asked.

"Yes, I think so. She went with her sister."

Lily smiled widely. "You're amazing. I can't believe you can really see and talk and do those things."

"You're amazing," I said. "Without you, I would've totally botched this. You were the one who knew what to say to her. You understood her. Only you."

"It's true," Laura agreed. "I might be able to sense their energy, and Sara here, well, my mind boggles at what she can do, but you, Lily, have a compassion that goes beyond all that. You reach out to help those so lost and far away. The power to see good in everyone is the truest gift."

"Laura, you can tell Mr. Himoff the rooms are now spirit free." I was giddy at the thought. I'd never done something like this without Lady Azura's help.

"No thanks to me. Whatever he pays me, I'm going to share with both of you."

"You don't need to do that," Lily said.

"Totally," I said. "This was your job."

Laura bent and picked up the small crystal. "Why

did you choose aragonite? It never would've occurred to me."

"It's for friendship, right?" Lily asked.

"Lady Azura said it has more power than that." I thought back. "It brings about acceptance and understanding."

For a moment, we both let the words sink in.

"Good thing Belinda left it behind for me." Lily twirled her hair nervously. "I'm sorry, Sara. I got crazy yesterday when you told me and—"

"No, I'm sorry," I said. "I didn't do it the right way, and I waited way too long."

"We both need a heavy dose of aragonite," Lily said, taking the crystal from Laura and slipping it in her jeans pocket.

"Agreed. Friends?"

"*Best* friends, silly."

"What about that ice cream down at the lake?" Laura suggested. "I could go for something cold."

As we headed toward the elevator, Lily checked her phone. "Kayla texted me a zillion times."

"Oh." I wasn't going to judge.

"She's starting to annoy me," Lily confided.

"Everything is all about her all the time."

"I can see that."

"My mom says Kayla always has to be center stage. She doesn't like her much."

"I thought you didn't care what your mom thinks," I teased.

"Sometimes she's right." Lily scrunched her nose. "Totally hate when that happens. She called you special that first day you moved in. Not that I didn't know that myself."

"You just didn't know how special," I joked.

"Otherworldly special," Lily said, linking arms with me as we ran down the lawn to meet Mrs. Randazzo and Angela by the lake.

A huge bonfire blazed on the beach, and both adults and teens milled about, roasting marshmallows and listening to two guys strum acoustic versions of pop songs on guitars. Despite the flames, the mountain air was cool, causing me to shiver in my sweat-soaked shirt. I didn't care. I was so happy to be outside under the star-studded sky.

Kayla and a boy were sharing ice cream on a bench made from a fallen log. She touched his shoulder with each exclamation as she told him a story. She waved to us, then returned to her tale.

Owen stood uncomfortably next to a thin, mop-haired man who could only be his father. His dad lectured to Mr. Himoff. Owen noticed me and crossed his eyes.

I crossed mine back. He *was* kind of nice.

"Hi, girls. Laura," Angela greeted us. "Look over there. The staff is setting up chairs for a wedding tomorrow. Isn't this the most romantic place? Can you imagine the gorgeous photos of the bride out there on those rocks?"

"Actually," Mr. Himoff said, making his way over to us, "we're doing the photos on a secluded point around the other side. There's a lone bench, and the view of the lake is magnificent. Big, big wedding."

"Not a problem," Laura said.

"Meaning?" Mr. Himoff asked.

"Meaning you're ready for a packed hotel."

"Our situation? It's solved?" He sounded surprised.

"The ghost is gone!" Lily exclaimed, clapping her hands in excitement. "Laura did it!"

"Really?" Mr. Himoff's gaze traveled around our

group. He wasn't sure how we knew all this, but he gave up trying to act proper. "Amazing! Congratulations!" He pumped Laura's hand. "Thank you."

Thank you, Laura mouthed to me and Lily as Mr. Himoff pulled her up toward the hotel to talk "business."

"I'm liking what I'm seeing," Mrs. Randazzo said. "Two best friends acting like best friends." She gathered us close and squeezed us in a group hug.

"Mom!" Lily wriggled away, even though I could've stayed that way longer. "Sara and I are getting ice cream. Come on, Sara." She took my hand.

As we walked off, Lily pulled the aragonite crystal from her jeans pocket. "What do we do with this? Should I keep it?"

"I gave it to you."

"But it's a friendship thing. Shouldn't there be two? We're both going to need help with understanding and acceptance if we're going to be doing this together," Lily pointed out.

"Doing what?"

"Seeing spirits. You and me."

"Together?" That soaring feeling was back again.

Lily nodded. "We're a team. You do the seeing and, I guess, I do the talking."

I pulled out my cell phone and dialed my house in Stellamar. It was late, but Lady Azura answered on the first ring.

"We're going to need another crystal!" I said, laughing into the phone. "Lily's part of our spirit thing too."

"All the way!" Lily added, her giggles blending with mine.

Epilogue

HELLIMAN HOUSE: Vacation Fun for Teens

By Angela Fiorini

Looking for a family-friendly resort that will impress the toughest guest, your teenager? Welcome to Helliman House, nestled in New York's picturesque Adirondack Mountains. This breathtaking, newly renovated resort has the fun and variety to interest smartphone-tapping teenagers as well as provide the rest of the family with an upscale good time.

Originally built in 1910 as a private summer retreat for a wealthy industrialist, Helliman House combines the rustic, old-world charm of a lakeside getaway with the modern fun that teens crave. New owner Grant Himoff has designed a retreat that meets the needs of all ages. The rooms in both the main building and the additions are spacious and feature large, flat-screen TVs, free wi-fi, minibars stocked with healthy snacks, and Jacuzzi tubs. Three on-site restaurants—ranging from the casual organic burger joint to an upscale Italian with to-die-for breadsticks—supply varied dining options.

"There were so many activities that we ran out of time to try them all," says teenager Sara Collins. An Olympic-size pool boasts a state-of-the-art waterslide and teen sunning area. A frozen yogurt stand and a frozen-lemonade bar are open poolside, and the "dive-in" screen broadcasts favorite TV shows and music videos right in the pool itself. The clear waters of Lake Hoby provide a roped-in swim area with trampolines, plus the opportunity to try water-skiing, canoeing, and paddleboarding. "I loved all the outdoors stuff," teen Owen Mann says. Teen hikes up nearby Mount Norma, a 5K run around the property, a scary movie night under the stars, a bonfire, and a teen dance are weekly features. A state-of-the-art game room is complete with video games galore and a mocktail bar.

However, unique to Helliman House is the most innovative draw of any hotel. Teen guests have the opportunity to interact with a newly hired on-staff spiritual adviser. Laura L'Angille, credited for ridding

Helliman House of ghosts rumored to haunt the halls, meets with teens to discover past lives, explore their latent psychic powers, and determine if romance and good grades are on the horizon. Although owner Himoff refutes a spiritual presence at the hotel, Laura leads teens on popular midnight walks to haunted locations on the storied grounds.

Whether your teens are looking for fun in the sun or moonlight thrills and chills, Helliman House is a winner! "My friend and I had the best vacation of our lives here," reports teen Lily Randazzo. "Not only was every day a surprise, but every hour!"

Want to know what happens to Sara next?

Here's a sneak peek at the next book in the series:

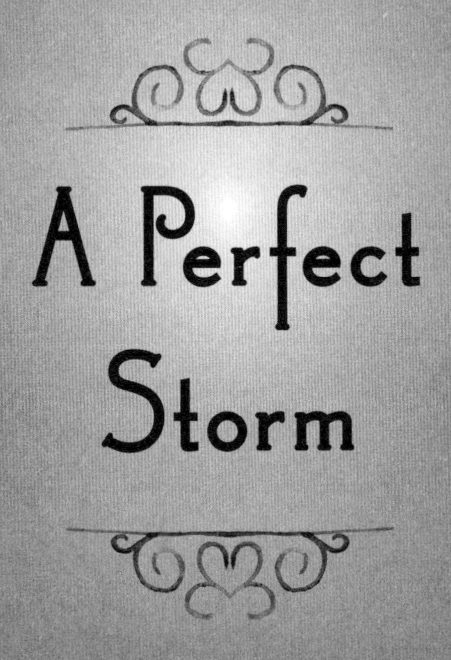

"It's only week three of school and already I'm bored with all the guys at Stellamar Middle School," my best friend Lily announced as she stirred the pool of butterscotch sauce at the bottom of her sundae glass.

"I know, right?" agreed Avery. She grimaced, her mouth revealing this month's band color, which was bright green. The bands she used for her braces tended to change color from one orthodontist appointment to the next. "That's the problem with living in a small town."

"It's true," sighed Marlee. "All the guys do at lunch-time this year is sit around in big packs talking about sports. They don't pay attention to any of us."

"Except Sara, here," said Avery, pointing at me with her spoon. "They notice you, because you give off that 'I'm not interested' vibe, which of course makes them interested. Can you teach me how to pull that off?"

"She pulls it off because she's actually not interested in any of them," Marlee joked, grinning at me. "Right, Sara? You're not crushing on anyone at school so far this year, right?"

"Earth to Sara," said Miranda, waving a hand back and forth in front of my face.

I jumped. Tried to focus on my friends. Tried to recover and act like I'd been paying attention, when really, I'd been staring out the window at the man standing on the sidewalk. He was dressed in strange clothing, unlike anything anyone else wore these days. Beneath his battered sailor hat I could see long, jet-black hair, loosely tied back in a ponytail. His pants were knee-length, his soiled blue coat fastened with big brass buttons, his thick-soled black shoes topped with large buckles.

Oh, and he shimmered slightly around the edges.

He was a spirit. A spirit I'd seen before, back at my house.

The question was, what was he doing *here*, outside Scoops Ice Cream Parlor? Had he come here to look for me?

Lily nudged me. "You okay?" she asked.

I smiled weakly. "I'm fine," I said. "I guess it's been a long week." But I wasn't that fine. I was having that familiar, unpleasant reaction, the one I thought I'd conquered. The tingling feeling that had started in my left foot was moving up my leg. The air around me had grown thick. The lights had grown dimmer, though I know it didn't seem that way to anyone except me.

My eyes darted toward the window again. The spirit wasn't paying any attention to me. I began to relax a little. Maybe he wasn't here to talk to me. He seemed to be muttering to himself. Rather abruptly, he spun on his heel and marched away, his head down, his hands clasped behind his back. Before he'd gone more than a few paces, he grew transparent. He shimmered for a moment, like a barbecue grill on a hot summer day, and then vanished.

Perhaps I should explain.

You know how kids sometimes talk about how they feel different, that no one understands them, that they just don't feel like they fit in sometimes?

Well, trust me. I win the prize. Because I really *am* different.

I can see spirits. Dead people.

I've seen spirits since I was little. Up until recently, I hadn't told anyone about it, not even my dad. But now he knew. And he'd moved us to this shore town in New Jersey the year before so we could live in a big, ramshackle Victorian house with Lady Azura, my great-grandmother. She had powers too, and she'd been helping me with my own powers. Which was handy, because her house was filled with spirits.

Only two other people know about my powers. One is a boy named Mason Meyer, the guy I have a crush on, though he doesn't know that. Mason goes to a different school. I had barely seen him since the summer had ended, but we did text a lot.

The other person who knows my secret is Lily. Lily Randazzo, my best friend.

Now, back in the ice cream shop, she saved me, by directing our friends' attention away from my weird, distracted behavior.

"You guys!" she hissed. "Turn around! Act natural! I just spotted Mason Meyer outside, and he's heading in here and he has a friend with him. A totally gorgeous friend."